P9-AER-907

TALES FROM THE

Haunted Mansion

TALES FROM THE
Haunted Mansion

VOLUME II
Midnight AT Madame Leota's

Transcribed by *John Esposito*
as told by mansion librarian *Amicus Arcane*
Illustrations by *Kelley Jones*

DISNEY PRESS
Los Angeles • New York

Printed in the United States of America

First Hardcover Edition, July 2017

5 7 9 10 8 6 4

FAC-020093-19330

ISBN 978-1-4847-1471-3

For more Disney Press fun, visit www.disneybooks.com

THIS LABEL APPLIES TO TEXT STOCK

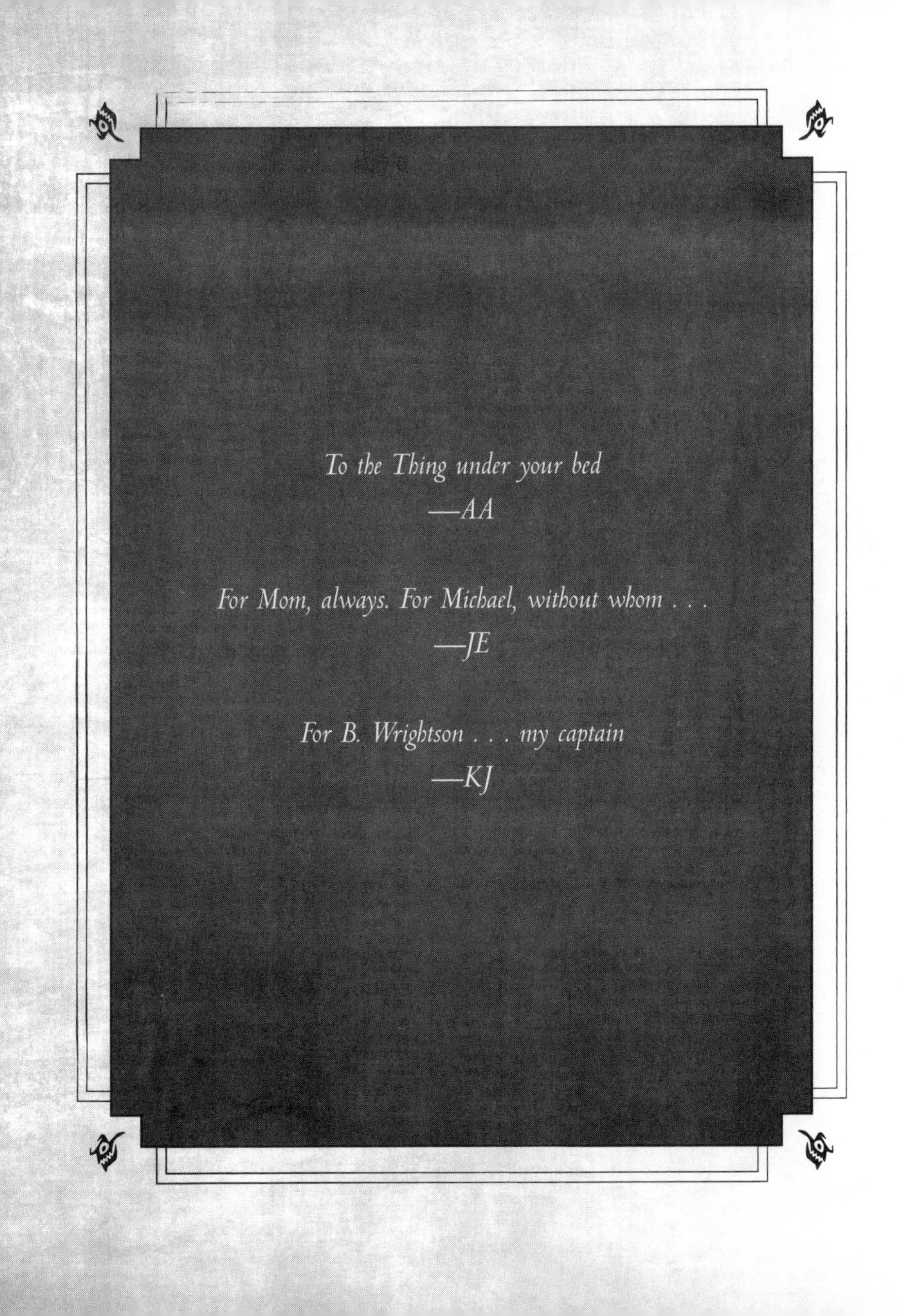

To the Thing under your bed

—AA

For Mom, always. For Michael, without whom . . .

—JE

For B. Wrightson . . . my captain

—KJ

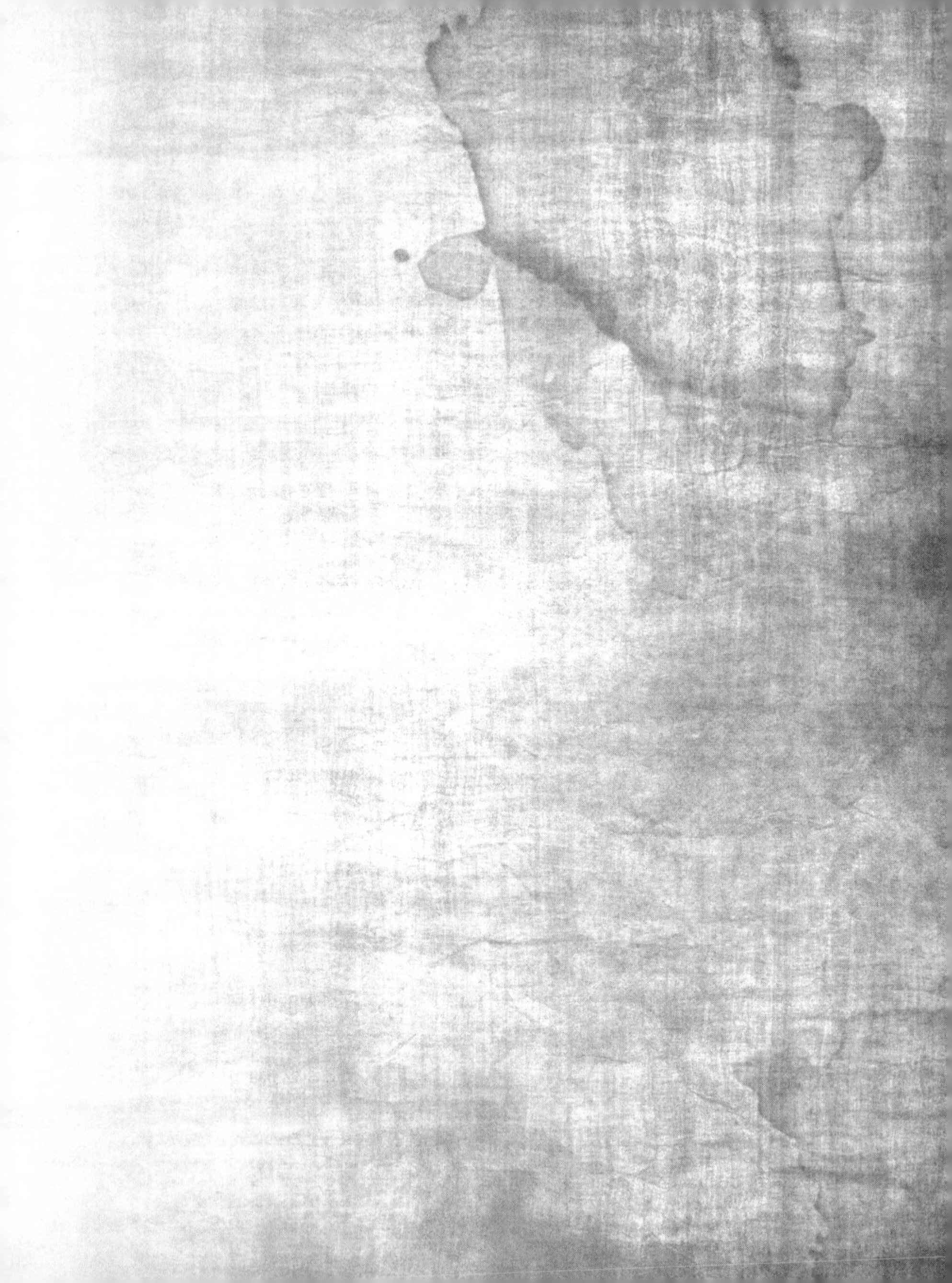

Very Unhappy Returns

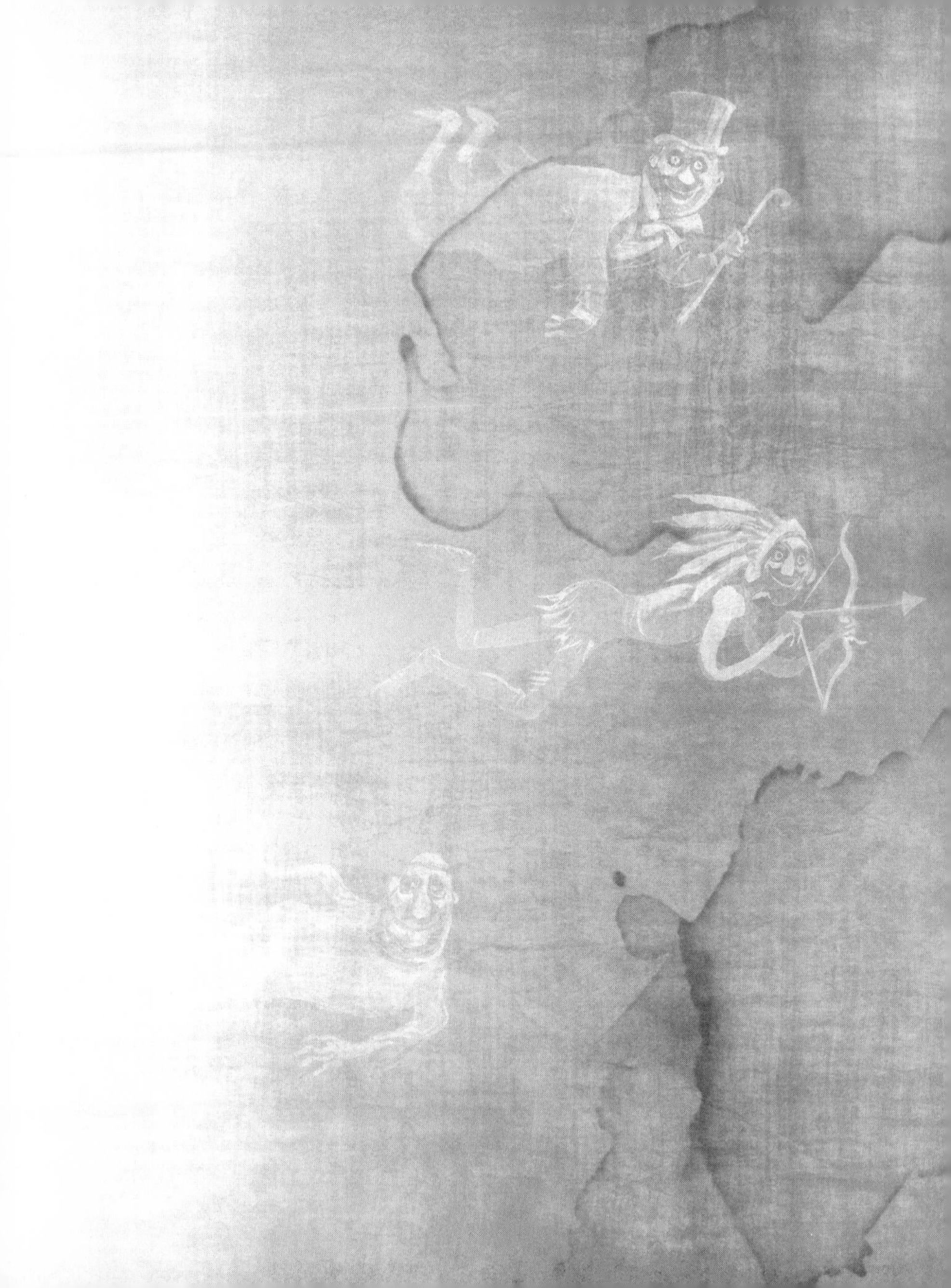

WHY HAVE YOU COME BACK?

This is no place for the living.

Did I not warn you of the danger?

Of the risks to your very soul?

If this does not sound familiar, I assume you skipped volume one. But do not fret, foolish reader; your utter lack of judgment shan't be held against you. Not yet, anyway.

To the others, I'm most unhappy to see you again—not because you've decided to return. Your sort—the sort that breathe—are always welcome in the domain of the dead. I'm only saddened because you got away in the first place. Rest assured I will not make the same mistake twice. As our happy hangman often says, "If at first you don't succeed, tie, tie again."

The book you now possess—or is it the other way around?—comes directly from the illustrious library of the haunted mansion, a repository of 999 chilling tales of mischief and the macabre. Every spirit has a story, you understand, some more terrifying than others, and I am the keeper of their tales.

In volume one, we met the Fearsome Foursome, four kids whose hobby it was to create scary stories—until they became embroiled in some scary tales of their own. And what frightening fictions they were, too.

For volume two, the mansion has opened its gates to a most unlikely visitor: a young man, still in the pink, as we say in the cemetery trade. His name is William, and he comes seeking an audience with Madame Leota, our "head" spiritualist.

Perhaps he's looking for a ghost. Or perchance he's looking to become one . . . an undertaking we're more than willing to facilitate.

Poor, misguided William. He doesn't believe in ghosts. Or ghouls. Or goblins.

What about you, dear reader? Do you believe?

You should.

You will.

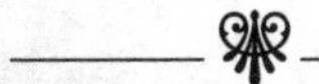

Chapter One

It was an annual event. A yearly tradition. *His* yearly tradition. It was how William always spent his sister's birthday, ever since she had died mysteriously in the night. This year, the festivities took place in a small cottage on a quiet street, thirteen miles off a forgotten highway. The porch was overrun by exotic plants, which roamed wild, as if they were children whose parents had abandoned them. This was the cottage where the weird old lady lived, the one the normal neighbors pointed fingers at behind her back because she was different. Because on Halloween she gave out live clown fish instead of candy corn. Because she had the guts to be different, and the rest of the world needed the weird ones to feel normal.

But there were rumors. And strange colored lights that, on certain evenings, seeped through the cracks of her venetian blinds. It was the home of a woman who claimed she could speak to the dead.

Within the walls of her modest parlor, stocked with the eccentricities of the trade—painted skulls, crystal balls, and beaded doorways—the middle-aged medium in the speckled bandana and matching peasant dress called forth spirits from the netherworld . . . or so she claimed. "Spirit, present thyself," commanded Madame Harriet. **What? You were expecting someone else? Patience, foolish reader. It's not yet midnight.**

Mediums—or spiritualists, as they're sometimes called—have been doing their thing since the 1800s, when the Fox sisters of New York first began channeling spirits for a fee. Séances quickly became a popular activity, even if 99 percent of these so-called spiritualists were frauds. But there's always that other 1 percent—the 1 percent William was interested in.

That was William Gaines, the up-and-coming writer. Perhaps you've heard of him? He just got his first article published on *The Unbeliever,* a site dedicated to explaining the unexplainable; to defining the unimaginable; to, putting it bluntly, sucking the magic out of life. In the past several years, William had participated in every paranormal activity imaginable, from tarot readings to voodoo rituals, and still, he felt no closer to his goal. Because, ironically, William *wanted* to believe. He was majoring in paranormal science at college, and spent his free time as a debunker, pulling the beards off department store Santa Clauses. Yet his one true desire in life was to speak to the dead.

Madame Harriet peered across the table, into William's steel-blue eyes. If she was trying to guess his thoughts, she had chosen the wrong face. "Did you bring it?" she asked. "A personal item belonging to the deceased?" William nodded. "Present it now."

William slid his hand into the pocket of his corduroy blazer. The personal item was stashed by his heart, a wholly appropriate location for so precious an heirloom.

The medium extended her left hand, palm up. "Hand me the item." William hesitated. Could she be trusted? Once a mischievous dreamer, William hadn't trusted anyone since the tragedy, not even his own parents. Death had taken his sister without warning, stolen her before her prime without a good-bye. The things left unsaid would haunt William's days and wreak havoc on his nights. Oh, the nights. The endless evenings that had cost him more than he'd care to admit. But all that torment might be forgiven if he could just talk to her one last time.

Madame Harriet spoke to the inanimate item in her palm. "Spirit, present thyself!" The table rattled. Had a spirit received her sympathetic vibrations? "Spirit, are you with us?"

In response, the table began to rise, one, two, three inches off the parlor floor. But William wasn't impressed. He'd seen every trick in the proverbial book.

Madame Harriet was watching with one eye open. She couldn't afford the negative feedback. Upping the ante, she began convulsing with violent spasms, at the same time emitting a long, drawn-out moan, the kind you'd have to practice to get right. William approved. *That* was impressive. Could she be the one?

Madame Harriet raised the personal item over her head, to the heavens, as it were. "The deceased is here with us now. Your loved one is . . ." She closed her eyes, as if to seal the deal. "Female."

William nodded. "Yes."

Madame Harriet continued. "She comes to me in song. Music. She enjoyed music." Again, William gestured in the affirmative. "And dancing. She liked to dance."

"Yes."

"She also loved to laugh, did she not? I hear laughter."

"Of course." William shifted in his chair, and the medium sensed his impertinence. He recognized what she was doing: a cold reading, no more than a series of educated guesses based on the evidence presented. The personal item was a girl's bracelet, so it wasn't much of a stretch to refer to the deceased as female. And most people like music, and where there's music, there's dancing. Nothing paranormal about that. And what kid didn't like to laugh?

Still, William would give her the benefit of the doubt. Because as cynical as he had become, there was that tiny part of him, buried alongside the boyish pranks and magic tricks of youth, that desperately wanted to believe. That *needed* to believe.

"Your doubts are clouding the session," warned Madame Harriet. "Do you wish to continue?"

"With apologies, I do."

"As you wish." Madame Harriet closed her eyes, awaiting the next message from "the beyond." "Your spirit, she had pets?"

William nodded, straining to hold his tongue. *Of course she had pets!*

Again, the medium needed to ramp up the action. She

slipped her hand under the table, discreetly pressing a button. Her chair bucked violently and there came about a series of lightning flashes, followed by a powerful wind. The French doors blasted open; the chandelier swayed wildly from the ceiling. "You have unleashed her wrath!" reported Madame Harriet. "The spirit is annoyed, Billy!"

William gasped, sitting up at full attention. Finally, the medium had gotten something right. His sister had *always* been annoyed about something when she was alive. But how did Madame Harriet know she called him Billy? A dose of emotion, as much as he'd allow, was starting to brew.

"Are you there, Sis? It's me. The little jerkoid. Say something if you're there."

Madame Harriet's left eye opened halfway. The "jerkoid" in her midst certainly wasn't little. William stood six foot two, with a slender physique and a mop of dirty-blond hair, like his sister. One might consider him a decent-looking fellow. Others had. If only he could remember how to smile . . .

"I am here, mine brother," responded Madame Harriet, channeling the deceased. ***"Mine." The dead are oh so formal.*** "Ask of me what you will, dear brother. Ask of me what you will!"

William had prepared his first question. "Are you—" As he began to speak, the wind died out, along with the lightning, as if God had pulled the plug. The chandelier steadied itself, and the table lost its buoyancy, dropping to the floor with a thump. Something had gone wrong. Had the dead broken contact? Or were there simpler and far more natural forces at work?

A middle-aged man with a potbelly draped over his belt strolled in through the French doors. "Apologies all around. We blew a fuse, sweetie. I'll check the breaker box." He was Madame Harriet's husband, Harry, on his way to the garage.

"Do not turn on the lights!" shouted Madame Harriet. "The spirits like it dark," she added for William's sake. But it was too late. Harry had located the breaker box. The power came on, juicing up the room. Once again, the French doors opened. But this time, the swaying chandelier brought an unwelcome light into the parlor. William could see everything. A giant fan was being used to blow open the doors; wires were swaying the chandelier; risers were lifting the table legs. It was unmercifully clear. Like the magic William had performed as a kid, it was all smoke and mirrors.

He reached across the table and retrieved his sister's bracelet, and Madame Harriet recognized the disappointment in his eyes. "Mediums provide a service," she said. "They tell people what they need to hear. Is that so wrong?"

"If you're seeking the truth, it is."

Madame Harriet smiled, touching his hand. "I hope you find it."

William left the cottage, thinking, *There has to be one—one authentic medium. Is that too much to ask?* William was determined to find her. Little did he know . . .

The world's most powerful medium was about to find him.

William was sitting on his own in the corner booth of the Tiki Restaurant for what would have been his sister's twentieth birthday. He spoke to no one that day; he didn't take his parents' calls or even their texts. He insisted no other voices intrude. The cake arrived—s'mores, her favorite—and along with a confused wait staff, William sang "Happy Birthday" to an empty chair. Strange guy, right? It should have gotten easier. Like a toothache, the pain was supposed to lessen over time. Eight years was a long wait. Would the feeling ever pass? If he could talk to her, it might.

It was getting late. A waitress packed the untouched cake in a to-go box, and William left the restaurant for the next phase of the morbid festivities.

The Eternal Grace Cemetery was one of the oldest, most distinguished boneyards in the land. William arrived at closing, unaware of the time. A bouquet of fresh flowers, left by his parents, no doubt, had been placed by his sister's grave. The headstone was adorned with an ornate granite sculpture of an angel in flight, her wings outstretched and her flowing hair appearing to change color in the moonlight. William sat down in the dirt, rearranging the flowers to his liking. They were pretty, like she had been. And in a day or two, they would die, like she had done. William removed the cake from the to-go box, then placed a slice in front of the grave and cut another for himself. "Happy birthday, Sis," he said to the angel's granite eyes. "Make a wish." He ate a forkful of s'mores, chewing mindlessly when . . . a shadow passed over the grave. William managed to swallow, looking around. There was nothing to see. He took another bite as he watched an elongated shadow coming closer, closer until a figure appeared, as if stepping through a blank doorway. William dropped his fork, startled. "Who's there?"

A tall elderly man was standing by the grave, an old lantern extended in his left hand. He was formally dressed, all in black, with a skull-like face topping an unnaturally thin frame. He wasn't a caretaker. William knew all of those. He might have been an undertaker, with himself as a client.

"Who are you?" inquired William.

"I am the librarian."

William snickered. "Funny place for one. You won't find many readers out here."

The librarian shifted the lantern, shedding light on the surrounding headstones. "But there are stories. More tales than even the grave can hold." He read the marker at William's feet. "You are celebrating an anniversary of sorts?"

"It's my sister's birthday." William extended the to-go box. "Care for some cake?"

"Thank you, no. I no longer have the stomach for it." **Literally.**

William pulled himself up by the base of the effigy. "Guess I lost track of the time." He bowed his head, pretending to pray, hoping the librarian would leave. But the stranger remained. "Look, would you mind giving me some privacy?"

"You wish to communicate with the deceased?"

"That's the general idea."

"Perhaps I can help." The librarian lifted the light, illuminating the angel's bust. "The dearly departed, she was a creature of flight?"

William nodded, fighting off tears. "In life, she was an angel. Except I didn't know it at the time."

"But you know it now."

"Doesn't do her much good, does it?"

"Oh, but you're wrong. Thoughts and prayers provide daily comfort to the dead."

William sniffled, wiping his nose on his sleeve. "I wanted to believe. More than you can imagine. I've been to every so-called clairvoyant and fortune-teller from here to Timbuktu, and you know what I found?"

"I'm *dying* to know."

"That none of it's true. Spirits, ghosts, goblins, the afterlife. It's a fairy tale. Except there is no happy ending."

The librarian shook his head. "That would be news to Leota."

William perked up. "Madame Leota?"

"You are familiar with her work?"

"I sure am. I did a paper on her. The world's greatest spiritualist. Even her skeptics would agree."

"Oh, yes, she is quite genuine," confirmed the librarian.

"She's also quite dead."

"A minor inconvenience, I assure you."

"You're not implying she's still alive? After all these years?"

"In a manner of speaking," the librarian said with a nod. "In a manner of speaking."

William couldn't help being amused. In fact, he almost

smiled. "You're a strange one," he said. He momentarily looked away. And when he turned back, the librarian had disappeared. What to make of the curious encounter? He waited several moments, but the stranger did not return. As William pivoted to leave—*Gasp!* The librarian was somehow standing beside him. "Whoa. Nice misdirection."

"Beg your pardon?"

"I studied magic as a kid," explained William. "Misdirection is a magician's best friend."

"I am not a magician. I told you, I am the librarian. I have *always* been the librarian." The mysterious stranger drifted onto a misty trail that seemingly led to nowhere. William couldn't let it go and took off after him.

"What you said back there, about Madame Leota. Or her namesake. I need to see her."

"I'm dreadfully sorry. You do not meet . . . the conditions."

William fumbled for his wallet. "Name your price. Anything. I'll pay it!"

The librarian refused the offer, pushing the wallet back toward William. "Payment comes in other forms."

"All right, tell me. Name the condition!"

"Death," responded the librarian. "*That* is the condition."

"I'm being serious."

"As am I." The librarian continued down the trail. And William continued to follow.

"Please, you have to help me!"

The librarian paused, hearing the desperation in William's voice, seeing the tortured look in his eyes.

Caw! Caw! From the highest branch of a gnarled tree, a raven, black as night, weighed in with its thoughts. The librarian listened. *Caw!* He considered it. *Caw!* He concurred, then turned to William. "Very well. Kindly step this way." He extended his lantern, revealing a zigzagging path formerly concealed by fog. William made a split decision to follow. What did he have to lose? **Except his heart, his lungs, his kidneys.**

"Where are we going?"

The librarian pointed. "Up there."

William looked up to see exactly where "there" was. His jaw almost hit the ground. **But "almost" doesn't count, except in "I almost made it out alive."** It couldn't be; it wasn't possible. He'd been to that cemetery a hundred times. He couldn't have missed it, but apparently he had: perched on a hill, overlooking the graveyard, stood a grand old mansion, enclosed by steel gates. But it wasn't just any old mansion. Its construct was born of a morbid mind; there was a discernible madness to its contradictory styles. Turrets jutted into the dark clouds, while oversized chess pieces adorned its roof. Scary, yet playful. The skeptic in William decided it was a trick—a high-powered projection. It was the only explanation.

"No trick," said the librarian, reading William's thoughts. He headed for a small gray structure, a mausoleum, with the surname ARCANE engraved over its archway. A stone door shifted open, welcoming them inside. The librarian glanced back at William. "Do you frighten easily?"

William shook his head. "No."

"Pity. I suppose we'll have to do it the hard way."

The librarian ducked his head and entered the mausoleum. William thought about turning back. The day had been a strange one, and it was about to get stranger. But he reminded himself, *This is for you, Sis,* lowered his head, and went inside. Immediately thereafter, the stone door returned to its first position, sealing the crypt. There was no turning back now.

The interior was old and musty, yet, like the librarian himself, it retained its dignity. An ornate stone sarcophagus was curiously vacant. Where had the body gone? Corpses don't usually go out for a stroll. But the Arcane crypt was anything but usual. William felt something nibble at his feet. He looked down. A plump rat was gnawing at his loafer.

William stomped his foot and the rat waddled off, not a care in the world, disappearing into a fissure in the wall.

The librarian continued moving, and William had to hustle just to keep up. They descended thirteen steps. When they hit bottom, the very air turned foul, and William sensed the walls closing in on him. They had entered a passage, unusually low and uncomfortably narrow.

"Mind your head," warned the librarian.

"I'll be fine," said William.

"I was talking to the head." The librarian shifted his lantern, bringing light to the passage. A human skull, wet with dew, was dangling just above them. The ceiling and the walls had been meticulously decorated with skeletal remains. Femurs jutted from the ceiling like stalactites; calcified fingers reached from the walls. Any sane person would have called it a night, but William had visited the catacombs in Paris and, as mentioned, did not scare easily. "Cute," he said. "What do you call this place?"

"A shortcut," replied the librarian.

A light appeared at the far end of the tunnel, and William caught glimpses of a more civilized setting. There were faint sounds, the morbid music of an old pipe organ. "This way, young sir," the librarian said, beckoning. William took a breath and followed him deeper into the tunnel.

For an instant, the air grew sharply cold, then the temperature slowly rose to be more hospitable. At the same time, the cobwebbed catacombs gave way to brick and mortar, and William found himself within the confines of a handsome hallway, where eyeballs stared from purple wallpaper and gargoyles with candles crackled their burning disapproval. William asked, "Is this Leota's house? Is this where she lived?"

"Resides, Master William. *Resides* is the word you're looking for."

"I don't understand."

"Before the night is over, you will. If true understanding is what you desire." The librarian continued down the hall.

William heard voices, a symphony of shrieks, crying out from somewhere in the mansion. He moved briskly, not to be left behind. Not because he was scared, mind you. "What on earth was that?"

"Merely the winds," replied the librarian.

"That wasn't the wind!" insisted William. "It sounded like people. I heard three distinct voices, crying out for help!"

The librarian concurred. "Oh. *That* sound. You're quite correct, sir. That would be Ezra, Phineas, and Gus. They've been with us for quite some time, though to be honest, they're always looking to hitch a ride out." He pointed onward. "This way."

The lantern fizzled out and the corridor went black. Losing his footing, William felt his way like a blind man, calling out to the librarian, "Sir! Sir!"

Light returned, and William found himself inside an enclosed room with no windows and no doors save for a high skylight that allowed a single moonbeam to shine like a spotlight on an old velvet chair. All four walls were lined with shelves overflowing with books—upright, on their sides, old, new, you name it. There was something oddly familiar, yet also discomforting, about this room. William stepped to a shelf, perusing a good number of the titles. Ghost stories, one and all.

The librarian appeared behind him, having replaced his lantern with a candelabrum. "Welcome to my library."

"My sister loved stories," said William. "The scarier, the better." The librarian reached for a book on the highest shelf. It floated down to his hand, VOLUME II engraved on its spine.

"What are you doing?" William asked.

"Selecting a tale." The librarian sank into the high-backed velvet chair and opened the old tome.

"I don't have time for that. What can you tell me about Madame Leota? Is there someone who carries on in her name? I need to know!"

The librarian looked up from the page. "And so you shall." He held William's gaze. "When you're ready."

"I'm ready now, sir."

"I think not," said the librarian before returning his attention to the written words.

Flames erupted from the fireplace. The library was preparing itself for a shivery tale. "All right," agreed William, "I'll listen." He planted himself in an antique chair opposite the librarian. "If that's what it takes to see Madame Leota. My name's Gaines, by the way. William Gaines."

The librarian didn't react to the name, because he already knew it. He felt obliged, however, to return the courtesy. "In life, I was known as Amicus Arcane."

"Arcane," repeated William, recognizing it from the crypt. "Very well, Mr. Arcane. I'm ready to hear your tale."

"And so you shall," said the librarian. He averted his unworldly eyes to the opening passage and, at William's behest, began to read.

Chapter Two

Step right up, foolish reader, don't be shy. The carnival's in town!

Most people never think about how a carnival gets where it's going. It simply arrives. And while it's true that these bizarre traveling shows, with their unusual delights and rickety rides, seem to spring up without an invitation, it's also true that a great many people do their level best to avoid them.

In fact, it's safe to say that many people do everything in their power to avoid them. The same people, mind you, who avoid roller coasters and horror stories.

Not <u>you</u>, of course.

When the carnival arrives, they remain indoors, holding their collective breath, waiting for the freak show to pass.

But the carnies themselves, they count on the masses. The rubes. The ones who feel a certain tingle when the tents go up, with sun-bleached signs promising weirdness and wonder.

So step right up! Don't be shy. There's a new show in town filled with magic and mayhem and who knows?

Maybe a little murder.

Please Remain Seated

The trolley car arrived with a shrieking halt, depositing the girls less than a mile from the old pier. They could already smell the mixed aromas of doughy hot pretzels and sweet cotton candy being airlifted by the cool autumn breeze. Those smells they had come to expect, along with others, less pleasing: the pungent vestige of a vomiting child; or the odious stench of wayward animals, human or otherwise, pausing to mark their territories. Then there were the electric fumes that lodged in your sinuses as the trolley left you where you paid to be left, going, going, gone. The two young girls now stood in a strange and mysterious world that not twenty-four hours earlier had looked as familiar as the constellations. But that was before *they* arrived.

In the black of night.

Bringing terror and delight.

The carnival was back in town. It came every fall, when the leaves turned golden, like people turn golden, when the promise of death is lurking within every shadow. It came with its weather-beaten tents, home to ten thousand delights, and its rickety rides, assembled with spit and a prayer, not a safety inspector in sight. All for the low, low price of . . . everything you've got in your pocket.

This is the promise of the traveling show: as funny as it is scary; as safe as it is dangerous. You might survive. You might not. But if you do, well, give yourself a good poke in the eye. You just cheated death.

The girls locked arms as they made their way up the wonky planks of the boardwalk stairs, a string of bouncing lights their first visual. A few more steps, and they could hear the sounds. Guests, screaming their lungs out and laughing just as loud: a curious combination of fear and delight. How closely those sensations are linked. Laughter and tears. Joy and sorrow. Life and death. Folks came from far and wide to experience the peculiar thrills of the carnival. Folks like Jane and Connie.

We often hear about how competitive girls can be. How they're sometimes catty, or jealous. But when it came to Jane and Connie, nothing could be further from the truth. A secret rivalry did not exist. Jane wished only the best for Connie. And Connie wished only the best for Jane. The best demise, that is. It would be perfectly acceptable if Connie's best friend croaked suddenly. Jane was far too gifted, too pretty, too well liked to live. But being Jane's best friend, Connie sincerely wished Jane's premature departure would be a painless one. **Now there's a best friend after my own nonbeating heart: putting someone else's death before her own.** And the traveling carnival was a perfect place to find death, if recent history had anything to say about it.

A season earlier, a girl had disappeared from one of the attractions. *Poof!* Gone. Just like that. At least that was what the rumors at school would have you believe. Francine was the girl's name, and according to middle school gossip, she ventured into the haunted house **(not everyone can afford a mansion, you know)**, never to be seen or heard from again. Of course, there was no evidence to support that assertion.

But that didn't stop the story of the kid who went missing inside the carnival haunted house ***(because they couldn't afford a mansion)*** from spreading like a disease. It was an urban legend. Even if you're unfamiliar with the term, it's almost certain you've heard or told one or two urban legends in your lifetime. These are stories involving strange occurrences that happened to someone nobody knows. It's all very convincing, except there's never a firsthand witness to the giant alligator living in the sewers of New York or the killer hiding in the attic. It's always something a friend of a friend's cousin's sister's boyfriend (who now lives in Canada) saw.

But Jane was a believer. It had to be true, because so many people said it was true. Connie, on the other hand, being of a less trusting nature, didn't buy a word of it, mostly because she wasn't there and didn't believe anything she couldn't see with her own two eyes. ***Oh, but I assure you, there are scores of things—some of them unimaginably terrible—brewing just below the surface of what we can see. One of which, I'm most pleased to inform you, is currently lurking under your bed.***

The story of the girl who went missing in a carnival haunted house ***(because they couldn't afford a mansion)*** had taken on near legendary status by the time the traveling carnival arrived for that season's tour of terror. If one thought about it, it made little sense. There would have been an investigation and big splashy news stories. But sense never figures into the equation when it comes to urban legends. Where's the fun in sense? It's like peeking behind the curtain at a magic show. It's all smoke and mirrors and sticky tape. **(Happy? Now you may get on with your own magically deprived lives.)**

"A winner every time!" shouted a vendor running a ball-toss game. He caught sight of Connie's angry peepers. "How about you, young lady? And your pretty friend?"

Ouch! That stung like a bee! No matter what Connie did, or how she did it, Jane would always be the pretty one. Even though they dressed the same—that night it was in matching blue gingham dresses—and their height and weight were almost exact, and their noses shared the same upturned shape, Jane would always be the pretty one. When Jane wasn't smiling or giggling, everyone said they could pass for sisters. So what made Jane the pretty one? It had to do with that elusive something special, a charming allure that some of us are born with. **And die with.** Putting it another way: Jane admired the colorful canopy of a butterfly's wings; Connie enjoyed removing those canopies. Slowly.

Jane saw only the good in people, even Connie. Especially Connie. **We'll get to that.** Which is why she had agreed to join her, three trolley stops from home, on that chilly Friday night Connie secretly hoped would be Jane's last.

"Step right up!" the vendor persisted. "I promise you, a winner every time!"

"What do you say, pretty one?" Connie poked Jane in the small of her back. "Wanna play?"

Jane returned a naturally disarming smile as she cleared the hair from Connie's eyes. The bigger eyes. The angry eyes. "I think you're the pretty one."

"You're a liar," said Connie. "But what the hey? I love you for it. Come on!" She grabbed Jane's hand, yanking her away from the booth. "Let's go find the freaks!" The girls giggled as they navigated through the meandering crowd, under and around couples and families, like two matching kites in the wind.

They were soon sucked into the eye of a strange yet marvelous storm in the center of the boardwalk. The Tent of 10,000 Unusual Delights was situated across from the carousal, where frozen horses ascended, mid-gallop, on brass Popsicle sticks to the unsettling score of the calliope. There were cries from the rickety roller coaster that built to screams of terror as it plunged into the pit of its first precipice and oohs and aahs from children pointing with delight as a nine-foot-tall clown drifted by on stilts. There was even an organ-grinder with a live monkey. **(Though the dead ones tend to be just as amusing.)**

Then there was the carnival barker, a man of three foot two, teeter-tottering in front of the massive tent, stained with blotches of heaven-knew-what, where a sun-bleached sign proclaimed a world of ten thousand unusual delights. **(There were actually thirty-seven unusual delights and thirteen eerie attractions, but who's counting?)**

"Step right up, one and all!" echoed the barker's voice through a megaphone. "Boys and girls, children of all ages! For a single quarter—a mere twenty-five cents—you will witness all manner of weird and wonderful delights that I, Mr. Majestick, have collected from around the globe. See . . . the living Gorgon, with a face so hideous one look can turn a man to stone. Attend . . . a tea party hosted by a living mummy. Marvel at . . . the living puppet-boy, whose face is that of a donkey. Take a dip in the stone bathtub of Captain Culpepper Clyne. Is he alive or is he dead? A quarter to me gets you in to see!" He pointed his stubby finger at Jane, spotting her within the crisscrossing crowd. "You, with the blank stare. Enter if you dare!"

Connie gave Jane a playful nudge. "He's talking to you,

pretty one." Jane planted her feet firmly on the pier, her shoulders tight, her body filled with angst. Something scared her. Something beyond the Tent of 10,000 Unusual Delights. "What are you looking at?"

"Nothing," lied Jane. "Let's go home."

"Not a chance. We just got here."

"I don't care. I want to leave. This place is a drag."

"Drag-shmag." Connie was done with the negotiations. She turned to see what Jane saw. ***Not much of a mystery if you've been paying attention, foolish reader.*** There, on the ledge of the pier, with a pitched roof and garish displays, stood a haunted attraction aptly called the Grim Grinning Ghost House. Pity, poor Jane. The attraction she had secretly hoped would never return, the villain of the urban legend, had come back. With a vengeance, as they say.

A festering side note to all you aficionados out there: This tale takes place in a not-so-distant past, when haunted attractions were of a more humble disposition. They did not include live performers in masks or high-tech gadgets or computer-enhanced holograms. The best you could hope for was a glow-in-the-dark mannequin to spring up out of the dark. Admission was a quarter, and the wait time was no wait time at all. Indeed, that was not a misprint. There was no

wait time. Not like the lines that accompany most rides today. Lines you might die just waiting in, but I digress . . .

Connie was growing impatient. She pounced. "Now I get it. You're afraid."

"Not true!"

"Oh yeah? Then what's on your arm?"

Jane didn't need to look. A sea of goose pimples had already arrived. "I-I'm cold, that's all."

"Or afraid," said Connie before upgrading her assessment. "Terrified's more like it!"

"Am not."

"Are too."

"Am not!"

"All right, prove it! We're doing the ghost house. Just like we said we would."

Jane got up on her toes, pretending to survey the attraction in all its spooky splendor. Really, she was focusing on the dark clouds rolling in behind it. Anything not to look. Not to see the laughing skeletons, purple and green, adorning the entrance, the shutters flapping open and shut along with the recorded screams. Jane was looking skyward to avoid seeing—*heaven forbid*—the infamous Francine flailing her arms in horror from the tallest triangular window before the house sucked her in like a clam. "I refuse to waste my last quarter on nonsense," said Jane, turning away.

Connie fished two quarters from her pocket. "I'll treat. How's that? Now what's your excuse?"

Jane yanked her arm from Connie's, just about the most aggressive thing she'd ever done. She regretted sneaking out her window to join her best friend in that don't-be-caught-dead-in part of town, where the most questionable of attractions, the traveling carnival, had laid stakes on an old pier above an ocean of cascading waves—waves that drove home this chilly reminder: Jane did not know how to swim.

Yes, the waves below the pier had grown restless. The gulls were restless, too, squawking as they circled. Something else had arrived: a force, unseen by most, strolling like a third shadow behind the girls. There was actual magic in the air. And magic comes in pairs. The first kind is born of light. It illuminates the good in our world. The second kind, the one you're most assuredly interested in, is the kind that festers in the dark, feeding off nightmares. You'll find both at the carnival. Which one you get depends on you.

This dark energy made Jane queasy; she needed to sit down. On the other hand, Connie was fueled by it. She tried offering—make that *insisting* that Jane try—a candy apple, her treat. Jane refused, instigating Connie's well-rehearsed pouty face. "Worried about your figure? Or afraid it might chip your perfect teeth?"

"No," replied Jane. "I don't like candy apples is all. Besides, you're the one with the perfect teeth."

"Nonsense. Everybody likes candy apples. Can't trust a kid who doesn't!"

"Then don't trust me!" Jane hated being bullied, especially by Connie.

Jane had timed the next trolley and was already making a move for the exit. Connie had to stop her from leaving. To take the trip inside the ghost house seemed like innocent fun, the kind you went to carnivals for. "Let's just watch for a while," suggested Connie. Jane shrugged. And from the safety rail with its peeled paint, they did just that. A pair of kids climbed into a black pod-like vehicle—**a Poison Pod, if you will**—with the number thirteen stenciled on the rear. The safety bar was lowered for them **(thank you very much)**, and the pod glided along iron rails, entering the black-as-coal entrance to the Grim Grinning Ghost House. "See? They went in. And they're younger than us. Eight or nine, at most."

"I'd say ten," said Jane. "They looked ten."

"That's still two years younger than us. A pair of ten-year-old squirts, brave enough to ride the ghost house without their mommies."

Jane gave it a moment's consideration. "I'm brave enough."

"Are you?" Connie snickered. "Let's face it. I'm the brave one. You're the pretty one. And you know what they say."

"What?" Jane had enough curiosity to risk hearing what would certainly be an unpleasant response. "What do they say?"

Connie unveiled a toothy grin, proving once again that smiles can be just as ugly as they can be pleasing. "Beauty fades." She handed the attendant two quarters, looking back at the pretty one. "Beauty fades."

Chapter Three

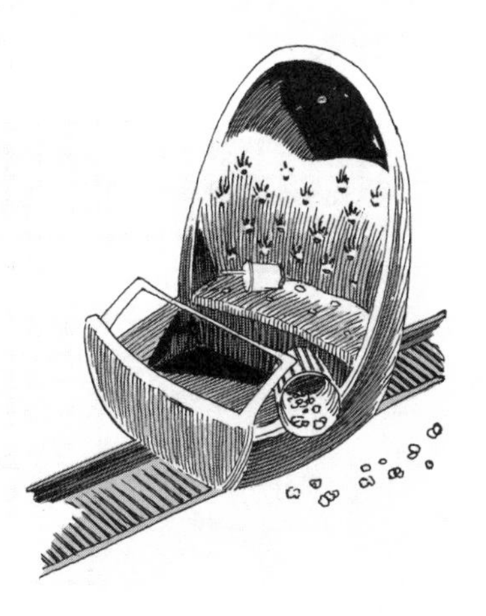

POD NUMBER THIRTEEN EMERGED from the Grim Grinning Ghost House empty, the guests, who might or might not have been ten, both gone. Had history repeated itself? With a trembling arm, Jane pointed out a splotch of red on the cushioned seat. "They disappeared! Look! There's blood on the seat!"

Connie was surprised, too—until she saw from the corner of her eye the same two kids barreling down the exit ramp. The probably-ten-year-olds from pod thirteen, one holding a red slushie. "There's your blood." Connie laughed. "Man alive, Janie. You're as gullible as they come."

"Am not."

"Are too."

Another pod jiggered into range, the seat turning on its own to greet them. The attendant motioned for the girls to board. Jane shook her head. "Seriously?" questioned Connie. "We came all the way across town just to chicken out. Besides"—Connie put the icing on top—"you owe me."

Jane's body stiffened. So Connie would be playing the "you owe me" card once more. How long would that go on? How much did she really owe Connie? Well, after you read this little flashback, you might argue that Jane owed Connie everything. Or at least her life, which is pretty much everything. **Oh, but it isn't.**

The debt Jane constantly found herself repaying came from an incident that happened at the beach the previous summer. That was the summer of '64, when beach movies played at the drive-in and a fabulous foursome from England invaded our shores. Now, you may ask, and rightly so, what a self-proclaimed nonswimmer, like Jane, was doing at a public beach, where, let's face it, you've got your sand and you've got your water. Lots and lots of water. And the only reason you put up with the sand is to get to the water. Well, Jane was there with her group, working on her tan. Connie was there, too, but not with the group. She despised the group, but that's beside the point. Jane went into the water up to her ankles. No harm in that. Then a little more. Mid-thigh. Then a little more. She was up to her waist, which was as far as she planned on going, when a six-foot wave knocked her over, and a vicious undertow carried her out to sea. Thank heavens for that girl no one liked. Connie. Her name was Connie.

You can guess the rest. Connie, being an excellent swimmer, dove in and saved Jane's life; there's no denying it. So how do you repay a debt like that? Well, you don't really. But if the someone who saved your life asks you to ride the haunted attraction at a traveling carnival, for crying out loud, stop your whining and climb aboard!

The attendant steadied the pod. "How many in your party?"

Connie looked back at Jane, hoping she had changed her mind, but she hadn't. "Just little ole me." The attendant reminded Connie not to lower the safety bar; the ghosts would lower it for her. She climbed into the pod, this one stenciled with the number two. But as it sputtered toward the entrance, Jane made a surprise move, scooting into the seat next to her. "Okay, you got me!"

Connie smiled. "I got you," she said, repeating the words with a more sinister tone. "I got you."

The pod blasted through a set of steel double doors, Jane and Connie gobbled up by the dark chasm of the carnival haunted house, where black lights and canned screams were the order of the night. All for a mere quarter, with no wait. Jane tilted her head back as the doors began to close, and through a sea of faces—young, old, cheering, jeering—she saw the barker pointing her way. "You'll be sorreeeeeey."

Blam! The doors closed and pod number two made its way twenty feet, stopped abruptly, and turned halfway. A purple light flickered on, and the girls were facing a witch stirring a potion in a cauldron. After the initial shock, they laughed. The display wasn't very convincing. The witch was clearly a store mannequin, with green poster paint flaking off her molded plastic face.

It had to get better. This couldn't be the same haunted house, could it? Not the one that claimed Francine, as per the urban legend.

The pod continued its journey, and Connie uttered the words Jane was thinking: "This had better get better."

It did not. ***Oh, but it will. Heh-heh!***

A plastic skeleton swooped down on a wire. It didn't even

have the courtesy to rattle. After that, a sheet on a stick, doubling as a ghost, said, "Boo." All very much your grandma's haunted house. Jane and Connie recognized the screams; they were the same ones from outside: fake, prerecorded, all part of the trickery. For Jane, it came as a great relief. If she had ever believed the urban legend before, it, too, had now turned to cheap molded plastic. Haunted houses didn't really exist. Not in amusement parks or in movies or in books. **But *you* know better, don't you?**

Jane's relief was short-lived. Connie had turned to face her, nose to perfect nose, the dark doing little to mute her angry eyes. "I have a secret," she began, her voice a gravelly hiss. "A terrible sssssssecret. You're the only one I can tell."

Jane shifted as far away from Connie as she could. Whatever Connie had to say, Jane wasn't sure she wanted to hear it anywhere, much less in the dark confines of a carnival ride, while she was trapped by a safety bar. "Can't it wait until the ride is over?"

"Boo!" A phantom wearing a top hat appeared before their pod, playing a funeral dirge on an organ. As a prop, it, too, left much to be desired, but as she was caught off guard, Jane unleashed a charitably realistic scream.

"Hold it together, Janie-girl. We're still best friends, aren't we?" Connie sounded like herself again, and Jane breathed a short sigh of relief.

"Yeah, sure, whatever you say."

Then the other voice returned. "Good. I must asssssk you not to judge."

"Okay, Con, you're starting to scare me."

"That'sssss sssswell," said the voice from Connie's mouth. "You should be ssssscared. Because I'm about to tell you sssssomething I haven't told anyone. That sssstory, the one about the kid . . . Francine. It happened, for real, right where we are. Want to know what *really* happened?"

"N-not particularly."

"Please, I have to get thissss off my chesssst or I might die!" The pod was slowing down, as if all its power was being drained by Connie's malevolent persona. They entered an unlit stretch, and Jane couldn't tell if Connie was close to her or far away, but she knew one thing for certain: Connie was easily the scariest thing on the ride. "You ssssee, I went to sssschool with Francine. Before I moved into town. Matter of fact, she's the reason I was forced to move in the firsssst place."

Jane felt a lump form in her throat, one she could not swallow. "The reason? Wh-what reason?"

"Before I came, there was a problem. In my lassssst town . . . they wanted to lock me up."

Jane didn't want to ask. But she had to. "Who's 'they'?"

"Doctorsssss."

"The doctors wanted to lock you up?"

Connie nodded. "In a padded room. All white. With a ssssslot in the door sssso they could watch me, day and night. Except it wasn't a room. It was a cage! A cage, all dresssssed in white."

"Stop trying to scare me!" shouted Jane. "What's that have to do with Francine?"

"Francine was my bessssst friend . . . before you. We did everything together. Even the carnival. You sssssee . . ." Connie paused. And when she continued, the anger spilled like bile from that unfamiliar voice. "Francine was the pretty one."

"You said that story wasn't true!"

"The sssssstory you heard, the one the kidsssss tell during lunch, on those white tables with their white bread sssssandwiches and their white, white milk . . . that sssssstory isn't true. I'm about to tell you what *really* happened, Janie-girl, the true story of what happened inside the Grim Grinning Ghost House, sssso listen up!"

Jane remained silent, not because she wanted to; it was

more that she was afraid of what Connie might do if she interrupted. Or rather, what the owner of the voice residing inside Connie's mouth might do. "Ssssso you'll let me finish, because I have to get thissss out fassssst."

Connie felt Jane nod in the dark. "She was afraid of the ghost housssse, too, and I told her. I told Francine there was nothing to be sssssscared of. It's all make-believe. I even paid for her ride. Ssssso she came. We rode the Poison Pod, like you and me are doing right now. And then sssssomething came over me. It was the mirrors, Janie-girl."

"What mirrors?"

"The mirrors! A hundred thousand reminders of who I had become." And for a split second, Connie sounded like her old self again.

"*Had* become? What are you talking about? You're Connie!"

"No, Jane." The other voice was back. Whispering. Hissing. Declaring. "I'm the ugly one."

With a *SWWATCH,* colored lights burst down from the rafters, a canopy of reds, blues, and greens, as the pod entered the heart of the ghost house—a magnificent hall of mirrors, some plain, some distorted. But in all of them were Connie and Jane, Jane and Connie. "I don't know what it wassss. Or who it wassss. The doctors, they called it another perssssonality, a sssssplit persssssonality, like I was ssssome-one else part of the time, sssssomeone I'm not. But what do doctors know? They don't want to cure you. All they want to do is lock you up!"

By then, Jane felt nauseous. "I need to get off. I'm going to be sick!" Her heart was beating a mile a minute. She was afraid. Of Connie. Or the new personality sitting beside her.

"That doctor," Connie continued, "he knew everything about nothing. He sssssaid I couldn't be cured, that ssssome people were born thisssss way. That I should live in a cage for what I did." She paused. "He didn't underssssstand. But you understand, don't you? Tell me you underssssstand or I'll do it again. I'll ssssslice you open like I sssssliced open Francine!"

Jane covered her ears. "Enough! I don't want to hear any more!" She would have pulled them off if she could have. **Not to worry, Janie-girl, around here you'll still be the pretty one.**

Jane pushed the safety bar as hard as she could. It didn't budge, and the mirrors kept coming, one after another, a universe of false promises: fat Connie and fat Jane, skinny Jane and skinny Connie, super-tall Connie and super-tall Jane, regular Connie and regular Jane . . . along with a third guest, propped up in the pod between them. A most *unwanted* guest.

Connie unleashed a shriek that was heard by no one,

because Jane's scream was three decibels louder. In that brief moment, the second most horrifying of her life, Jane saw a body slumped between them—the corpse of Francine, from the urban legend. She drooled black ooze, and then Jane saw something else: an image that would haunt her for the rest of her days.

The dead girl in the mirror opened her bulging eyes and curled her lips, forming a smile more terrible than Connie's. Francine was wearing a hideous gaping grin and was staring, wild-eyed, at the two girls when—

CLICK! Out went the lights. The ghost house was thrown into complete darkness once more. Jane let out a full-blooded wail those prerecorded screams could only dream to emulate. And with a burst of adrenaline, she forced up the safety bar and bolted from the pod.

Poor Janie-girl. She didn't even get to hear Connie's laugh, see her doubled over in the pod, the tears steaming down her cheeks. "Jane, wait! What are you doing? It was a joke!" You see, Connie had known all about the smiling mannequin—she had been to the carnival the night before—and made up the accompanying tale about murdering Francine to scare the living daylights out of her best friend. **Ah, a girl after my own spleen!**

Connie had succeeded, only too well. The pretty one ran off into the dark, leaving Connie with a twinge of regret. She was being playful, or so she thought. But the carnival's dark energy recognized Connie as one of its own. It recognized and embraced her.

The pod *rrrrrr*ed to a stop. There was a malfunction, a delay, soliciting groans throughout the ride. A ghostly voice spewed instructions from the loudspeakers: "Unfriendly spirits have interrupted our tour. Please remain seated in your Poison Pod. Your tour of terror will continue momentarily."

Connie stood up, trying to spot her friend. "Jane? Janie-girl? Come back! It was a joke!" she cried. But Jane didn't answer. "It was a joke," she said again in a whisper. A moment later, the pod bucked and the ride came back to life. The other pods remained on course, but pod number two took a frightening detour. *What's going on?* Connie thought. The pod picked up speed and flew off the tracks, gliding into a restricted area where a flashing red sign warned DO NOT ENTER: GO BACK!

Connie found herself traveling through an altogether different hall of mirrors, one not open to the public, its reflections less playful, as the truth can sometimes be. A deformed soul glared back at the girl with the angry eyes, smiling its toothy grimace. Connie barely had the chance to scream as the pod raced directly at it, blasting through and shattering the mirror.

Meanwhile, Jane followed a path of emergency exit lights back to the pier and burst outside, screaming bloody murder. Faces in the crowd turned to stare, and the barker turned to gloat. Jane had become the ghost house's star attraction. The louder she screamed, the more quarters he collected. The thing that ultimately silenced her was pod two, rolling out of the Grim Grinning Ghost House. The seat was empty.

Connie had disappeared.

Jane watched all night from a paint-chipped rail as the police combed the area, expanding their search to the water below. For her, the myth of childhood ended on the pier that night. The girl who'd saved her life was never found. When at last the sun rose and the sweepers came out of hiding, the carnival lifted its stakes, folded its tents, removed its clown white, and gathered its goods. On to the next town, maybe even yours, with ten thousand wonders to behold. And a new urban legend to be told.

Fifty years went by before Jane paid another visit to a traveling carnival. Because in truth, she never really had to. A night hadn't passed since that fateful October when she didn't find herself trapped in its hall of mirrors, not a solitary sleepless evening in ten thousand when she didn't hear its sounds, taste its flavors, smell its aromas. All the terror she could ever want.

For the mere price of a quarter.

Now in her golden years, Jane was able to reflect on a good and charitable life. But evil rarely gives up without a fight.

Fifty Octobers on, a traveling carnival arrived in the town where Jane now lived—a town without a pier—planting its stakes in a vast field where vegetation no longer grew. It was Jane's granddaughter, Emily, who begged her grandmother to take her to the show that Saturday so she could see its wonders, smell its smells. Experience its fear. After a day of resistance, with Jane making every counteroffer she could think of—the zoo, the movies, the mall—she eventually caved. But it had very little to do with her granddaughter. The day had come and Jane knew it. It was time.

To return.

They got there at dusk, grandmother and granddaughter, clasping hands. "Let's go on the Ferris wheel!" Emily turned for her grandmother's approval. Jane stood like a statue, her features chiseled fear. "Grandma, what's wrong?" The rides, the games, the vendors. They were the same. A brand-new carnival hadn't come to town. It was exactly the same. The vendors calling out to the rubes to play their games and taste their goods hadn't aged a day. Pacing outside the Tent of 10,000 Unusual Delights, the barker spotted her through the crowd. "Welcome back," he said to the old lady in the bifocals. "I'd know those peepers fifty years away."

For an instant, Jane's heart stopped—she was literally dead—but then her granddaughter rattled her hand. "Check it out! A cheesy old haunted house!" She tugged Jane's arm. "We have to do it!" And she ran off to get in line.

"Emily, wait!" Jane took off after her granddaughter, slowing down when the rickety attraction came into range. The Grim Grinning Ghost House had been waiting for her by the edge of a lonely field. Emily was already in line, an empty pod puttering her way. "Em, please. It might not be safe."

"We came all this way. Don't tell me you're chicken."

That made Jane smile. *Chicken.* Some insults stood the test of time. "Yeah, your old grandma's a chicken. Come on. I'll buy you a candy apple."

Jane extended her hand, but her granddaughter didn't take it. A candy apple, as good as they are, couldn't compare to the retro thrills of the Grim Grinning Ghost House. "That's okay, Gram, I'll go alone. See ya on the other side . . . chicken."

Emily laughed as the attendant swiveled the pod for her to board, and Jane felt her breath leave her body.

It was pod number two.

As the pod rode the rails toward the entrance, Jane ran alongside and, at the last second, leaped in next to Emily, who scooted over with delight. "So you're not so chicken after all." The safety bar lowered and the pod blasted through the double doors. Jane glanced back, seeing for the second time in her life the barker pointing a pudgy digit her way. "You'll be sorreeeeey!"

And for the second time in her life, Jane knew he was right.

The pod puttered through the haunted attraction, which was as unrefreshed as it had been in the past. The department store witch stirred her plastic cauldron; the flying sheet said "boo"; the skeletons still refused to rattle. And Emily groaned. "Guess I should have listened."

"Just enjoy the ride," said Jane. "It'll be over soon."

"How do you know?"

"Oh, just a feeling."

Just then, the ride *rrrrr*ed to a crawl and the announcer's voice bellowed from the speakers: "Please remain seated." Jane's granddaughter shifted anxiously, pushing up on the safety bar. Jane took her hand. "Relax, it'll start up in a minute."

"What if it doesn't? Grandma, I'm scared."

"There's nothing to be afraid of, angel. I'm here."

Emily rested her head on her grandmother's lap as the announcer continued his prerecorded spiel: "Unfriendly spirits have interrupted our tour. Please remain seated in your Poison Pod. Your tour of terror will continue momentarily." Two, three, four minutes passed before the pod sprang to life, crawling like a beetle to the heart of the attraction. Emily was still frightened, and refused to look up.

Pod number two glided into the hall of mirrors, greeted by a rainbow burst of color. Jane had anticipated a third figure, the fake Francine, glaring back from the glass. But she *hadn't* expected the chilled feeling she got when an unseen presence entered the pod.

Emily felt it, too. "Grandma? It's cold."

"Don't look, baby, it will be over soon." But Jane *had* to look; this was fifty years coming. In the mirror, she saw a third figure seated in the pod: a girl with angry eyes, forever twelve, wearing a blue gingham dress and a well-remembered grin. The figure laughed at the old lady with the bifocals, as if the mirrors hadn't already done their job. "What'd I tell you, Janie-girl? Beauty fadesssss."

Chapter Four

William was staring into the fireplace, lost in thought about his childhood—a childhood that passed too quickly. "I haven't been to a carnival in years. Since I was a kid. I used to go with my . . ."

"Sister?"

The mere mention of the deceased lured him back to the present. "You're wasting my time, Mr. Arcane. That story had nothing to do with Madame Leota."

"Patience, Master William. All will be revealed in time."

"I'm ready now!"

"In time," repeated the librarian. He rose to his feet,

running his hand across a bookshelf. "Every spirit has a story. This spirit you seek . . . what was her story?"

"Why?"

"All tales interest me." He ran his spindly fingers across the bindings, the books his favored companions. "Human and inhuman alike."

"Tales interested her, too. The scarier, the better. My sister was a natural-born storyteller."

The librarian glanced down at the book he had been reading. At once, the pages started turning on their own. But William was unimpressed. He knew how most tricks were accomplished, and although this one had him stumped, it was still a trick, all the same. The pages came to a halt on the next chapter, the librarian grinning his devilish approval. "Oh, yes, I believe you'll find our next tale—"

"No more tales. The only thing I'm interested in finding is information about Madame Leota. Did she really speak with the dead?"

"Always. But first, our second tale."

"Thanks, but no thanks, Mr. Arcane. I'm going to find someone who can actually help me." And with that, William walked toward a long dark tunnel.

"Once you leave the library, I cannot guarantee your safety."

"I can take care of myself, thank you very much."

"Master William!" said the librarian. William paused. "Are you betrothed?"

"Excuse me?"

"Have you taken a wife?"

"I know what 'betrothed' means." William shook his head. "No. I'm not married."

"Then I beseech you: stay clear of the attic. Our resident bride, Constance, is always on the lookout for a new suitor."

"The attic," William repeated to himself. *That's where the secret lies. The attic is where I'll find out more about Madame Leota.* "Thanks for the advice, Mr. Arcane." He removed a candle from a sconce and proceeded into the tunnel.

The temperature dropped almost instantly. William moved the candle back and forth, noticing that the walls were swelling, as if the house itself was breathing. It wasn't hard to imagine being trapped inside the guts of a giant being, to believe that this strange mansion wasn't built from brick and mortar. Rather, it was a living entity that accepted you in, opening its doors like the jaws of a giant organism, only to spit you out into who knew where? A swamp? The cemetery? The thought almost brought a smile to his face. Almost. **But "almost" doesn't count, except in "I almost didn't get hit by** *that truck.*" But houses weren't alive. Secret passages didn't breathe, and doorways didn't swallow guests. Where this passage would lead, though, was anyone's guess, and William found himself wishing he were back inside the confines of the library, along with its host, Amicus Arcane.

Halos of warm light flickered just ahead. Wall sconces, those grinning gargoyles, were now a welcome presence. William made it out of the passage, into a corridor. This was more like it. Windows overlooked a moonlit landscape, and the paneled walls were lined with portraits. He panned with the candle, eyeing the peculiar artwork. At the same time, he could feel the artwork eyeing him.

"There you are, Master William."

He lurched back, practically jumping out of his skin. The librarian was standing in front of him, holding volume two in one hand, a candlestick in the other. "Oh, I didn't mean to frighten you . . . prematurely. The real chills come later."

William located his breath, followed by his voice. "The portraits. More tricks, Mr. Arcane?"

"I'm certain I don't understand."

"Oh, I'm certain you do. I'm getting the distinct feeling I'm in for a letdown."

The librarian appeared genuinely perplexed. "I assure

you, I can vouch for your satisfaction just as I can vouch for your very soul."

"You mean your soul, don't you? Vouch for *your* very soul."

"If you say so."

William gazed up at the final portrait, that of a gentlemanly-looking fellow holding a lantern and wearing a high-collared opera cape. A most curious aspect was the two canine teeth—fangs, actually—protruding from his mouth. And the eyes were closed, as if he was asleep standing up.

"This portrait, it interests you?" asked the librarian.

"Who is he? The owner?"

"Hades, no." The librarian explained: "Like most of our residents, he is a retiree. We have nine hundred ninety-nine happy haunts here, but there's room for a thousand. Care to book early?"

"Residents?" William chuckled. "I haven't seen a living soul since I got here." At that remark, the gentleman in the portrait opened his eyes. William jumped back, startled. "Whoa! Great effect. How did you do that?"

"Do what?"

"The eyes. They just popped open."

The librarian tucked volume two under his arm, then reached into his vest and checked the time on his pocket watch. "Yes, he should be rising for his first meal of the day."

"Just rising? It's the dead of night."

"The Count has always been a night person."

"The Count? Give me a break. You're not trying to tell me . . . what? That this guy's a vampire?"

"And has been for centuries." The librarian closed his eyes in wistful remembrance. "How he came to our attention is a story in and of itself."

"I told you, no more stories. Unless they involve Leota."

The librarian closed his watch with a snap. "We have time, Master William."

"Time for what?"

"To learn why you're here." The librarian shifted the candlestick, throwing additional light onto the portrait, and for just a flash, William saw an altogether different form inside the frame. The Count had momentarily taken on the appearance of a wolf. William knew from the old legends that vampires were shape-shifters, having the ability to transform into various creatures, including wolves, rats, and bats.

"Okay, I'll listen. If it'll get me closer to the truth."

"Oh, it will, Master William." The librarian opened the book, the pages flipping to the next chapter. "It most assuredly will."

Chapter Five

Vampires are real. They exist, and have since the beginning of time. Are you aware that every culture on earth has fostered a belief in vampires, those undead beings that rise nightly to drink blood from the living? It's true. Absolutely. Unequivocally. And when we discover life on other planets, vampires will likely be there, too.

The traits are the same. Before TV or the Internet existed, cases of vampirism swept across continents. How can we explain it? Mass hallucination? A message in a bottle? Or the more reasonable . . .

They exist. They always have.

No one claims Frankenstein's creation was real. Or that a certain Dr. Jekyll literally transformed into a certain Mr. Hyde. But Count Dracula, a.k.a. Vlad the Impaler? He's fact. Look him up. We'll wait.

You see, Dracula existed—pardon me, exists—as surely as you or I. But it's not my intent to frighten you, foolish reader. Simply to inform you, to pass along some helpful information. To begin with, vampires rarely attack the living. That is, unless they're thirsty. Oh, but they're always thirsty.

Hmmm. Perhaps that wasn't so helpful.

Of course, there are myriad ways to ward off an attack. For starters, vampires despise garlic. Crosses generally drive them batty. They melt like cheese when sunlight hits them, and driving a wooden stake through the heart of one leaves a permanent scar, though the practice should generally be restricted to experienced vampire hunters. But your best defense comes from identifying the threat before anything happens—which can be difficult. You see, vampires look just like—and might be—anybody we know. Our friends. Our neighbors. And sometimes . . . even members of our own family.

Blood Relatives

"Oh, man, my country bites!" Ernie said, procrastinating building his exhibit for the International Day school fair. "Romania? Who gets Romania?" Despite his protests, Ernie had gotten Romania for a reason: it was part of his lineage. Ernie was a quarter Romanian on his father's side. So Romania it was—which struck him as a total bummer. Team France was building an Eiffel Tower out of matchsticks; Team China, the Great Wall of Papier-Mâché. Claudia Coats, over at Team Caribbean, claimed she hailed from pirate stock. But Romania? "What in the world are they famous for?"

"Transylvania, idiot!" shouted Vicky van Sloan from Team Holland. "And vampires."

"I thought vampires lived in the Pacific Northwest."

"And you, Ernie Looper, live under a rock. Transylvania is famous for bloodsuckers." She stomped her wooden shoes for emphasis.

"Lovely," sighed Ernie. "There goes *that* grade." It wasn't the first time he'd felt ashamed of his heritage. The genetic gifts just kept on giving. Let's see: there was the beak-like nose he got from his father's side, the severe widow's peak that formed a V over his caterpillar eyebrows, and the pasty complexion that couldn't hold a tan. But worse than all those combined was a red birthmark on his right cheek that looked like spattered jam. His mom called it a strawberry mark, because, well, she was his mom. The lovelies at school, not being his mom, had other names for it, like Cherry Cheek, Dot o' Rot, Tic-Tac-Toe Face, and the less eloquent but far more popular Puke Puss. *Thanks for that one, Loopers.* But we are who we are. Life is as simple and as complicated as that.

As far as Ernie knew, he wasn't related to anyone cool. No movie stars, no Ben Franklins. The Loopers' one claim to fame was a delicatessen established by his great-great-grandfather when he immigrated to east New York. According to a menu in an old family scrapbook, the specialty of the house was an item called blood pudding. *Mmmm. That sounds tasty.*

Making her rounds, Ms. Fisher, the history teacher, stopped by Ernie's booth. She was sweet and caring, one of those teachers who encouraged students to share her enthusiasm for—lord help us—world history. She slipped her glasses to the tip of her nose, gazing with care at Ernie's display. "How's Romania coming along?"

Ernie was having trouble matching her enthusiasm. "The Taj Mahal would have been nicer."

"Don't focus on what you don't have. Focus on what makes your country great. The culture, the people. Something in your history."

He told her about his great-great-grandfather's blood pudding. And the eternally uplifting Ms. Fisher displayed an expression bordering on disgust. "Hmmm. Sounds interesting." She removed her glasses, as if that might erase the image "blood pudding" had just conjured in her mind. "How about going further back? To a time before your great-great-grandfather. To the past glories of Romania and her people."

"How do I do that?"

Ms. Fisher flashed her fake disappointed face. "What do I always say?"

" 'Eat on your own time'?"

"Yes, I say that, too. But I also say, 'Research is the key to unlocking your potential.' You have the tools. It's as simple as clicking a mouse, Ernie Looper. Uncover your past. I have a hunch you'll like what you find. But find it fast. Your project's due on Friday." She side-stepped over to the next exhibit, where Kyle McGivers claimed he was related to Benjamin Franklin.

Ernie thought about it. The tools were at his fingertips. There were 101 know-who-you-are websites to choose from. You could trace your lineage back to a cave if you wanted to. And that was what scared Ernie the most. What if the Loopers had always been as un-special as he suspected? What if he was the latest in a long, embarrassing line of Ernies, getting picked on at Transylvania High for generations? As pathetic as his dad, a plumber. Or his mom, who worked in a cubicle. Or his big sister, who couldn't land a prom date even after she paid for the tickets. Yes, the truth could be scary. But as someone famous—*definitely not a Looper*—once said, "The truth shall set you free." Maybe Ms. Fisher was right. Maybe, just maybe, there was something in his past. A prince or a knight or . . . who knew? Maybe even a count.

As soon as school ended, Ernie rushed to the library **(No, not ours)** to use its computer, because it was way faster. Delving into a brief history of Romania, he discovered a country rich in culture and cuisine, with a long history of battles and alliances as complex as any. But the real reward came when he stopped by WHO-B-U? and found that Looper wasn't even his original surname. His great-great-grandfather changed it from Lupescu when he arrived at Ellis Island: "Lup" from the Latin *lupus,* meaning "wolf," the full translation being "son of the wolf." A promising start. But wait, there's more! There was even a family crest, a symbol that looked like something you'd see on the chest of a superhero, featuring the head of a snarling wolf, all-conquering—something to be proud of.

Where had he seen it before?

From there, it was easy to trace his ancestral line. To his shock, Ernie learned that he had royal blood flowing through his Looper veins. He was a direct descendant of a count—an actual count. Can you believe it? **Of course you can. You know what you're reading.** He clicked on a name in the "past notables" section and, because photos didn't exist back then, a painting appeared. Not that a camera would have done much good. **(We'll get to why later.)** An image of the Count appeared. Ernie had inherited his nose and his widow's peak, but not his eyes. The Count's eyes were like burning coals, searing through the monitor. Scrolling farther down, Ernie clicked on a Fun Fact and grinned. *Wait till Vicky van Sloan hears this.* It said that the Count was believed to be a vampire.

Of course, vampires weren't real. They were the products of cheesy books and even cheesier movies. But it was a great kick to imagine being related to one. *Call me Puke Puss one more time and I'll suck you dry!* If only. If only.

That night, during dinner, Ernie mentioned what he had learned, but the conversation was cut short by his mother. "A vampire? That's a bit much, don't you think?"

"Maybe nowadays. But the world was a superstitious place back then. The big takeaway from all this is that we're related to a count, an actual count." Ernie clapped his hands in amazement. "Imagine. Us, of all people!"

His father dropped his fork. "What's that supposed to mean? 'Us, of all people'?"

"Well, I'm just saying. You're a plumber, Mom works in a cubicle. We don't exactly live in a castle."

That did it. His father slammed his fists on the table,

and Ernie could have sworn he saw actual steam coming out of his ears. "Sounds to me like you're ashamed of us!" Ernie didn't even hear his father. He was still lost in thoughts of his infamous lineage.

"Did you know that our name *isn't* Looper? It's Lupescu. Our real name's Lupescu."

Seeing the anger in her husband's eyes, Ernie's mother ended the conversation. "Excuse me, Your Royal Highness, but that's enough. Clear the table, then start working on your homework."

His sister looked up from her phone, a borderline miracle. "Smooth."

Ernie cleared the table and excused himself to his room, where his project was waiting. As he put the finishing touches on his topographical map of Romania, he remembered where he'd seen the family crest before. It was on an old crate in the attic that his father said was filled with junk. Was it possible that the dullest family in America kept a secret hidden in the attic? Ernie decided to find out.

It was a few minutes after lights-out when he tiptoed into the hall, pulled down a retractable ladder from the ceiling, and climbed into the attic. The Looper attic, like most, was loaded with unnecessary keepsakes: old records, old magazines, old games. **Old corpses. (Sorry, wrong attic.)** Ernie crawled along creaky floorboards, passing holiday decorations, until he came upon the wooden crate, exactly where he remembered it to be. It was bound with steel chains and secured by a medieval-looking lock, the kind you might use to keep a particularly unpleasant something from getting out. The Lupescu crest was emblazoned on top.

Ernie gave the lock a jiggle. *Hey, you don't know if you don't try,* he thought. No good. Luckily, he found a rusty crowbar mixed in with some tools. He inserted the flat end into the lock and, with a good heave, broke it in two, releasing the chains.

Ah, the moment of truth. Ernie wedged the bar in the seal and pried open the crate. *Whoosh!* The stench was rancid. And being a plumber's son, Ernie was well acquainted with rancidness. But this smell was singularly different. He'd never been around a dead body before, yet somehow Ernie knew: the crate smelled like death.

He continued to raise the lid, which creaked like it was supposed to. He was expecting old photo albums or, at best, an electric train set. But who locks up their toy trains and old photos with a chain? As far as he could tell, the crate contained nothing of value. Just some outdated evening wear—a suit and a cloak—along with a smattering of gray dust at the bottom. But then he saw something else mixed in with the dust. At first, Ernie thought it was a twig. He examined it, deciding it looked more like a rib. He poked at the tip. "Ow!" A red bead swelled from his fingertip, and before he could do what came naturally, which was to suckle it, several blood drops landed in the crate.

On the dust.

Ernie fled the attic in a hurry, squeezing his bleeding finger as he made a mad dash for the second-floor bathroom. He was looking for the first aid kit when a solid four knocks at the door interrupted. "You okay in there?" It was his mother.

"Fine, Mom. I'm just, you know, going to the bathroom."

"Ernie, there's blood in the hallway. What's going on? Open this door!" *Thud! Thud! Thud! Thud!* Fearing the next four thuds might wake up his dad, Ernie opened the door, and in rushed his mom. "What on earth happened?"

"Nothing. It's not serious. Just a paper cut."

She took a gander at the wound. "That must have been some piece of paper." A crimson trail was oozing down the side of his finger.

"I'll put some peroxide—"

"No!" she protested. "Peroxide retards the healing process." She took hold of Ernie's protracted finger, bringing it to her lips. "An old Transylvanian cure passed down from Grandpa Looper," she said before sucking away the excess.

Ernie felt queasy. It didn't take a genius to connect the dots. His mother had a taste for the red stuff. But she wasn't a member of the undead. She couldn't be. For starters, she liked extra garlic on her pizza. And she didn't sleep in a coffin. She slept on her half of a queen-size bed. A pain in the neck, maybe, but a vampire she was not.

She tended to his finger. "Now go to bed." But as she leaned in for a kiss good night, Ernie backed away. "I vant to suck your blood," she said in her best Bela Lugosi accent. "What? You thought I was a vampire?"

"N-no." A nervous chuckle followed. *Not you,* he thought. *But what about Dad?*

She kissed his forehead. "Tomorrow's a school day. Make like a bat and fly off to bed."

Ernie did as instructed, going straight to bed. But sleep didn't come anytime soon. His finger was still throbbing, the blood acting as a transmitter, though he didn't know it.

Something was happening in the attic. Ernie could sense it. Should he go up and see? For our story's sake, yes, definitely! But Ernie wasn't reading this story; he was living it. So he wisely chose to stay in bed.

But we'll go up and check it out for him.

Within the eldritch crate, the gray dust had been nurtured by Ernie's blood and was already hardening, reconstituting into bones. Within minutes, a full-sized skeleton had formed. Muscles grew, adhering to bone. Veins and arteries found their way to a tumorous beating muscle inside the chest. *Thump-thump, thump-thump.* A wormlike organism slithered into an empty cranium, evolving into a brain. Liquefied skin moved deliberately across the limbs, like a candle burning backward. Eyes took root inside the hollow sockets. The same searing eyes from the painting.

A living, breathing entity was now lying in the crate, taking in small sips of air. It did not know where it was or what century it had woken up to. All it understood was the hunger it felt. The unquenchable thirst. It needed sustenance to survive.

It needed human blood.

—

A thunk from the attic shook Ernie out of a sound sleep. He sat up quickly, taking his own pulse, relieved to know he was still alive. Again, the best course of action was to stay in bed.

"Aahhooooooo!"

He heard that. A mournful howl, like that of a wolf. Maybe it was Buttons, the dog from next door.

"Aahhoooo-aahhooooooo!"

Ernie climbed out of bed, went straight to his window, and checked the neighbor's yard. Buttons wasn't outside; she was in the window across from his bedroom, not howling, not barking. The dog was trembling. Staring at the top of Ernie's house. He smushed his face against the glass. What did she see? He opened his window and stuck his head outside. Wet flurries hit the back of his neck. Maybe Buttons was intrigued by the first snow of the season. No, it was something more. He twisted his head, looking straight up the wall. What Ernie saw defied all rational thought.

The figure of a man had slithered out of the attic vent and was crawling, headfirst, down the side of the house, his hands clinging to the green siding like claws, a black cape unfurling behind him like the wings of a giant bat.

Ernie yanked his head inside and slammed down the window, as if that would help. He could never unsee what he had just seen, and he was already anticipating a lifetime of nightmares. His first thought was to warn his family. He raced to his door and swung it open to find a figure standing in the hall. It was his father.

"Why are you up?" Ernie's father asked.

Again, Ernie checked his pulse. Still alive. "I saw something!"

"Calm down."

"No! You don't understand. I saw a man climb down the side of the house. He had hands like a lizard. And wings like a bat!"

"You were dreaming."

"No, I wasn't!"

"Yes, you were. It was all a bad dream, honey," said Ernie's mom, joining them outside his room. She moved between them, placing an arm around Ernie's shoulder, and walked him back to bed, leaving her husband standing in the hallway.

A few minutes after settling under the covers, Ernie decided she was right. **(Don't tell your mother, but moms usually are.)** It must have been a dream. How could it not have been? Ernie closed his eyes, taking another shot at sleep. The church bells had begun to chime from Town Square, and as the first snow fell past his window, Ernie entered that state between dreams and reality, thinking about International Day. About Romania. About Transylvania. About the first snow of the season. And about the thing—the *vampire*—that had crawled down the side of his house, like a bat crawling down the side of a cave. And with this impending horror now loose in the night, Ernie knew that his life would never be the same again. . . .

Chapter Six

A veil of darkness made its way across Town Square. Flurries had graduated to flakes, and the sidewalk was carpeted in white, untouched by footsteps, human or otherwise. It was late. The church at the far end of the street confirmed it, its Gothic chimes announcing midnight. Chelsea Browning's shift had come to an end. She bid her manager good night and exited the twenty-four-hour convenience store, greeting the snow with a smile. Not so long ago, she would have been hoping for a snow day. But Chelsea was no longer a schoolgirl. These days, the snow represented runny noses and hazardous road conditions.

She raised her woolen scarf above her ears and began her nightly walk. Her car was parked farther away than usual. After hearing the weather report, Chelsea had moved it under a trestle during her ten o'clock break.

Smart move. Less snow to clear.

Her boots were the first to penetrate the new snow, *scrunch-scrunch-scrunch.* She was the sole person in the square, which was not unusual, considering the hour. It was, by all accounts, a safe area. But lately Chelsea had gotten to thinking: it only took one thing—a single, solitary horrible something—to turn a good area into one that's forever bad.

Tonight was the night for that one thing.

A dark figure was standing in the middle of the road. He hadn't been there a second before, and he'd appeared to come out of nowhere. Chelsea turned away to avoid staring. But the one glimpse she'd managed to get tripled her heart rate, and her breath appeared as intermittent puffs of smoke in the night air.

The stranger had no visible breath.

And there was another detail, one she might have missed had her senses not been telling her to be on guard.

The surrounding snow was untouched, without a solitary

footstep, as if the stranger had been set down from above.

Chelsea shuddered. She had to keep moving. Have her keys ready. Get to her car, lock all doors!

Don't make it look like you're running, she thought. The trestle was just ahead, its cave-like entrance drooling large icicles. She could see her car, bathed in shadows. Almost there.

A quick glance back.

The stranger remained inert, the surrounding snow undisturbed.

And yet he was closer.

Chelsea began to run, no longer concerned about what the stranger might think. She had never known true danger. Had never tasted genuine fear. The next day, she might laugh it off. But on that night, it was something to scream about.

She slid across the icy pavement, making it under the trestle. She disengaged the locks, the alarm chirping, her car a stone's throw away. And as she reached for the door handle . . . a large shadow passed over her from above. She craned her neck to see. What was it?

"Do not be afraid," came an accented voice from behind her.

Chelsea spun around. The stranger before her was dressed

all in black, not a splotch of color on his person. She could see his face now. He was a middle-aged man, with strong aquiline features. His hair, jet-black, was swept back, and came to a point in the center of his brow, forming a prominent widow's peak. His eyebrows were bushy black caterpillars; his complexion a ghostly blue pallor.

Chelsea managed to squeak out, "Please don't hurt me."

The stranger extended his hand as an old-school gentleman would, unveiling the inner lining of his cape, as red as fresh blood. He smiled, and Chelsea could see two sharp canines protruding from his upper lip. "You need not fear me," he said as he glided her way. "I am a friend."

His eyes—***the ones from the painting***—penetrated hers. Chelsea teetered back and forth, ensnared by his hypnotic glare, a power he had perfected five-hundred years before she was born. She was now his puppet, and would prove her obedience by removing her scarf. The stranger outstretched his arms, his cape unfurling into wings. "You must feed me, Chelsea. If you don't, I will perish."

"But . . . I have no food."

The stranger cupped the back of her neck, holding Chelsea's head firmly in place. "You *are* my food." He surveyed her throat and located her jugular vein. How many years had it been since he had feasted? The stranger did not know. Nor did he care. It was neither good nor evil that dictated his diabolical desires. It was a thirst. A hunger, unendurable. "I need to feed," he said, and bit down, his razor-like canines puncturing flesh like the skin of an apple, Chelsea's heart pumping as he feasted, sending blood back up to the jugular . . . as the stranger satisfied his unearthly appetite.

Ernie shuffled into the kitchen, a latecomer to the breakfast table. From the window he could see about three inches of snow covering the back porch. He checked his phone, hoping for a snow day. *Three inches? Gimme a break,* he thought. On TV, the morning news was already reporting the brutal attack in town. The victim, a convenience store clerk, was receiving a transfusion at Saint Joe's Medical Center. A doctor with a thick foreign accent called her condition hypovolemic shock, caused by substantial blood loss. **Vampires love when doctors explain away their eating habits in clinical terms.** Ernie's mother switched off the set. "Hey, I was watching that!" he said.

"Not while we're eating, you're not."

His father lowered his coffee mug. "Hate to break it to

you, bud, but school's open for business. Scarf down breakfast and get a move on. Chop-chop!"

But for some bizarre reason, Ernie had lost his appetite.

A banner featuring that year's International Day theme, "It's a Small World," hung from the gymnasium bleachers. **You can add the "after all" part if you'd like. You know you want to.** But the talk was all about Chelsea Browning. "I heard her eyes were sucked out of her head," was the gossip coming from the Italian booth. "Not true," chimed in someone from Poland. "They found her heart in the snow. Still beating!"

But the only one with an actual clue was the girl in the wooden shoes. "It was a vampire," declared Vicky van Sloan, receiving chuckles from the surrounding booths—except for Romania. Ernie wasn't laughing. And when Vicky took a five-minute break, he took one, too, following her across the gym.

"Hey, Vic."

"Ernie Looper. How's life?"

"It's a living."

She liked that one, so she smiled. "I'm heading over to the Greek booth. I hear the baklava's to die for."

"Baklava? What's that?"

"It's dessert. You'll thank me later."

Okay, so he wasn't Don Juan, or even Johnny Depp, but Ernie knew an invitation from a girl when he heard one. So he joined her in "Greece," pretending to enjoy the foreign pastry. But baklava was the last thing on Ernie's mind. He waited for the right moment before broaching the subject. "That thing you said back there . . ."

"What did I say back there?"

"About the girl. You said she was attacked by a vampire."

"You heard correctly. My opa—it's what I call my grandfather—he works at the hospital. He was there when the paramedics brought her in. She had two puncture wounds on her neck. Very little blood. That's Vampires 101."

"But . . . vampires don't exist. I mean, not really."

"Aha! That's their greatest strength. Nonbelievers like you, Ernie Looper, going around spreading their propaganda. Vampires love that."

"I'm sorry, but it's crazy." He laughed nervously.

Vicky put the brakes on. "My grandfather isn't crazy! He's the sanest person I know. He dedicated his whole life to the study of such things."

"What such things?"

"The things adults no longer believe." She kept walking. So Ernie kept following.

"Vicky, wait! Let's say I believe."

She looked down, trying to suppress a smile. "Then I'd say you're smarter than you look. But I kinda already knew that."

He skipped right over the compliment. "Okay. Let's say I was a vampire."

"You?" She giggled at the thought.

"Let's just say. For argument's sake. What would you do about it?"

"All vampires must be destroyed. It's international law."

"How?"

Vicky tapped her head, coming up with some answers. "I'm not exactly an expert, but Opa taught me the basics. A wooden stake through the heart is still the most popular method. Then you've got sunlight. That does them in."

"For real?"

"For real. You ever see a splotch of melted cheese wearing a bow tie? It was probably a vampire."

"Sick."

"You think so. You want to hear something even sicker?" Ernie nodded. "They have no reflection. Not in mirrors. Or cameras. They can't even take a selfie." That reminded her . . . Vicky took out her phone and snapped a selfie. "One good thing," she continued, "they can't enter a home unless they're invited. It's part of the rules."

"Vampires have rules?"

Vicky nodded. "Like we don't? You have to wait twenty minutes after you eat to go swimming, don't you? That's a rule. But there is a silver lining to all this, including silver."

"I'm listening."

"If the head vampire is destroyed, then every person they turned into a vampire goes back to normal. Assuming they were normal in the first place."

"And if it isn't destroyed?"

"Then every person that becomes a vampire keeps turning people into vampires. And so on and so on. Until the whole world becomes theirs." Ernie grew paler than he already was. "Hey, what's wrong with you?"

"I don't feel so well."

"You need the nurse?"

"I need a stake."

Assuming he meant the other kind, Vicky pointed to a nearby booth. "You're in luck. China has pepper steak."

Ernie rubbed his belly. "Think I'll pass." He staggered back to his own booth, feeling awful from his widow's peak to his toes. The topographical map of Romania was on display. Was it Ernie's fault? Had he unwittingly unleashed a vampire on his town? And if so, how long would it take for its foul contagion to spread across nations, like the ones represented in the gym? Ernie looked around at the other booths. **It's a small world, after all.**

Over the next three days, reports of three more attacks dominated the headlines. Same details. Puncture marks. Loss of blood. *You know, Vampires 101.* Ernie had purposely kept away from the attic. *What you don't see can't hurt you.* But his conscience had done a number on him. Something dreadful was happening, something he had started. Yet who'd believe such a thing? Vicky van Sloan, perhaps. Ernie needed a plan. Vampires weren't stupid. They enjoyed the wisdom of the ages. During wood shop an idea came to him. He'd been putting the final touches on his wall sconce—basically a basket for mail—when a solution presented itself.

It took only a few minutes on the lathe before—eureka!—he had converted his wall sconce into a wooden stake . . . that also held mail. His teacher promptly converted his A to a D, but it was worth sacrificing his place on the principal's list to rid the world of evil.

Ernie knew something was wrong the moment he walked through the door. There was an aura of evil about the dining room. Okay, that's a little dramatic. But there was a mysterious stranger at the head of the table, where his father usually sat. The stranger stood, as a gentleman does when someone new enters a room. He was tall, about six foot six. And handsome, in an unconventional way. "You must be Ernest," he said with an eastern European accent.

Ernie felt his legs give way to gravity. He knew at once that the fiend who had drained Chelsea Browning and others of their blood had been invited into his home as a dinner guest. Ernie's sister was seated to the stranger's left, entranced by his signet ring, which featured an engraving of the Lupescu crest. His father was fiddling with a bottle of Bordeaux. Ernie's mother rushed in from the kitchen, collecting Ernie, taking his arm in hers. "We have a surprise guest!"

The stranger met them halfway, extending his hand. It was the same hand Ernie had seen clinging to the side of the house, and he refused to shake it. "So. Who invited you?"

His father stepped forward, a stern look in his eyes. "Ernie, shake the Count's hand."

The Count! It was confirmed, though the long black cape had given Ernie a clue; this wasn't one of his dad's pals from the plumber's union. The Count shook his hand with a grip like a steel vise. It was quick, but long enough for Ernie to understand. The Count could crush him. Along with the rest of the family if he so desired.

Ernie's mother broke the silence. "This is amazing! We're related to royalty. A real live count." Ernie's mother smiled. "Honey, pop open the wine!"

The Count bowed modestly. "My title is an anachronism. I am merely your humble guest." He noticed an item in Ernie's left hand. "What is that you have?"

"A wall sconce," replied Ernie. "It also holds mail."

"May I see?" The Count reached out to take it, and Ernie shifted it behind his back, in a somewhat rude manner.

His mother was mortified. "Ernie, what's gotten into you?"

With little choice, Ernie handed over the sconce. The Count examined it, intrigued, turning it over, poking the sharp tip. "Take caution, young Ernest. This could break the skin, no?" He handed it back to Ernie.

"I-I'll be careful."

"I know you will." The Count nodded.

Ernie's father beckoned them to the table. "Don't be rude. Let the Count sit down. He must be bushed from all that travel."

"The Count flew all night to get here," added Ernie's mom. Under different circumstances, Ernie might have laughed. But there was nothing funny about this situation. Thinking fast, he excused himself, saying he had to wash up before dinner. "Allow me to hold that for you, Ernest," said the Count, pointing to the sconce. "We wouldn't want you to hurt yourself."

"I'll keep it, thanks!" Ernie scooted from the dining room, ducking into the first-floor bathroom, where he put in a frantic call to Vicky and, in one long breath, told her everything. At first she politely listened. And then she laughed. Ernie was irate. "You of all people. I thought you believed!"

"I do. It's just . . . you need proof."

"Okay. What kind of proof?"

Vicky thought about it. "I know, I know. Take a picture! If nobody's in it, then the somebody that's a nobody is most likely the somebody you're looking for!"

It took Ernie a moment to process what she had said. *(Just like you.)* But he sort of got the idea. "Okay, then what?"

"Destroy him. For the sake of humanity. Drive that wall sconce through his blackened heart!"

Ernie hung up the phone, and a moment later, the doorknob jiggled. Ernie backed away, tripping and landing on the toilet. What if the fiend was right outside? Having left Ernie's entire family at the dining room table, sucked dry? There was a knock, followed by more jiggling. "Yo, dingbat, you fall in in there?" It was his sister.

"I'll be right out!" Ernie splashed some water on his face, looking up at his reflection in the mirror, for perhaps the last time. Was he up to the task? Could his thirteen-year-old brain outwit a being who'd outlasted centuries? It was almost time to find out.

He returned to the dining room just as a platter was being placed in the center of the table. It was a specialty from the old country, brought by the Count. It was called *blood pudding.*

The night a vampire shows up at your house for dinner should be the worst night of your life. But for Ernie, it might have been the best. The dinner conversation saw to that. What the Count had to say about Transylvania blew away his online research. The Count exhibited the most magnetic personality

Ernie had ever encountered. Admittedly, middle school students weren't renowned for their magnetic personalities, but still . . . The Count spoke proudly of the old country. The battles their ancestors had fought in the name of freedom. They were a noble class Ernie suddenly felt a part of. It was easy to believe by looking at him. Ernie shared the Count's nose, his eyebrows, his widow's peak.

And even . . .

"The mark of the Lupescu." The Count was pointing to the birthmark on Ernie's cheek, a trait of the royal family, he explained, dating back centuries. "We Lupescus have a right to be proud." The Count loosened his tie and lowered his collar, and tears welled in Ernie's eyes. A matching birthmark was on the Count's chest. For the first time, the dots on Ernie's cheek were no longer an embarrassment. They were a birthright. He was a Lupescu, the blood of a warrior pulsing through his veins.

As the evening drew to a close, Ernie's dad asked the Count about his plans. "America is the land of opportunity," noted the Count. "It will also be the land of my retirement."

"You're much too young to retire."

The Count replied, "I am considerably older than I appear."

The remark ripped Ernie out of the moment, propelling him back to his mission. He took out his cell, on the pretense of taking a family picture. "Smile!" The Count went along, grinning at the strange modern device, at which point Ernie caught a glimpse of his canines.

Seeing Ernie's face, his sister asked, "What's wrong?"

"Nothing," lied Ernie. "It's all good." But it wasn't. Because when he looked at his phone, the Count's image wasn't there.

Ernie spent all night holed up in the attic, waiting for the Count to return from his nightly feeding. The lethal wall sconce (that also held mail) was in his quavering hands. The Count had to return to the crate, his resting place, before sunrise. But what would Ernie do when he saw him? Complete the mission? Drive a wooden wall sconce into the beating heart of a man he now respected? Even admired? Blood is blood, after all. Or . . .

There was another option. A second choice came up during a last-minute call to Vicky. Either way, Ernie was about to find out.

There was a crunch, followed by a wrenching sound. Ernie lowered his blanket and saw the vent being yanked out of the wall. Flecks of snow entered the attic, followed by a shadow, spilling into the aperture like black ink, rising, finding form. The vampire had returned and was preparing to enter his crate when Ernie stepped out of hiding. The Count smiled when he saw him, like a favorite uncle might, which only made it harder. "Ernest, what have you got there?"

"A wall sconce."

"That also holds mail," added the Count, completing the thought.

Ernie nodded. "It also kills vampires." He took a breath, fighting his emotions. "You see, I know what you are."

"You are correct," said the Count. "I am a vampire, and have been for over five hundred years." He pointed to his chest, showing Ernie where to strike. "You would be doing me a favor. It is a curse to live eternally, to walk the earth feeding on the blood of the innocent. Your blood gave me life again. You must set me free." The Count opened his shirt, giving Ernie a clean target to his heart. It was the birthmark, that infernal thing that had plagued Ernie his entire life.

The Count remained immobile as Ernie crossed the attic, then placed the tip of the lethal wall sconce against the vampire's chest. "Do it," ordered the Count. Ernie could still hear Vicky's words: *All vampires must be destroyed!* He closed his eyes, unable to look, as he prepared to finish the deed. "Do it!" But . . . but . . .

"I can't." Ernie dropped the wall sconce and backed away. The Count was family.

"You must! I command you!"

"I can't!" Ernie could see the weariness in the Count's eyes. Perhaps he'd been at it too long. Perhaps he really did want it to end. "Is it true, what you said about wanting to retire?"

The Count nodded. "It is so."

"That's good, very good!" Ernie felt a twinge of relief trickling in. "I have a friend—her name's Vicky. And Vicky, she talked to her grandfather. He's sort of an expert in the field. And he said there's a place that might take you in. A place where people won't bother you as long as you stop bothering people."

The old vampire wasn't buying it. "Strike now! There is no place for my kind in this world."

"But there is! A mansion—built for your kind and others . . . in your condition. You can go there now. Before sunrise. Or . . ." Ernie picked up the wall sconce, taking aim at the vampire's heart. This time he meant business. "I can't allow you to drain anyone else."

The Count lowered the weapon with one finger. "How would I find such a place?"

Ernie smiled. "Just follow the moon. You follow it to an old graveyard, the Eternal Grace Cemetery. From there, the mansion will find you."

The Count looked back at his blood relative with pride. "You are a noble man, Ernest Lupescu."

"Looper. The name's Ernie Looper."

The Count granted him a deep, respectful bow, then turned and faced the breached vent. He raised his arms above his shoulders. The cape transformed, silk becoming wings. The Count's body shrank and sprouted hair, and before Ernie's astonished gaze, an oversized bat was flapping in its place, the vampire's searing eyes, now in miniature, looking back at Ernie.

"Safe travels," said Ernie, bidding him farewell.

The bat fluttered out through the vent. Ernie rushed over to watch it fly across a vast winter landscape by the light of a blue moon. The bat would eventually find its way to an old cemetery. And from there, a gated mansion on a hill.

—

Later in the week, Ernie's sleepy little town returned to normal. And on the first real snow day, he hung out with Vicky van Sloan, boasting about his mom, who worked in a cubicle, and his dad, the best plumber in town. They laughed until it hurt, and made snow angels until they shivered.

The same night, Chelsea Browning returned to her job at the convenience store. During her ten o'clock break, she drank her first customer. And within a month, their sleepy little town was infested with vampires. . . .

Chapter Seven

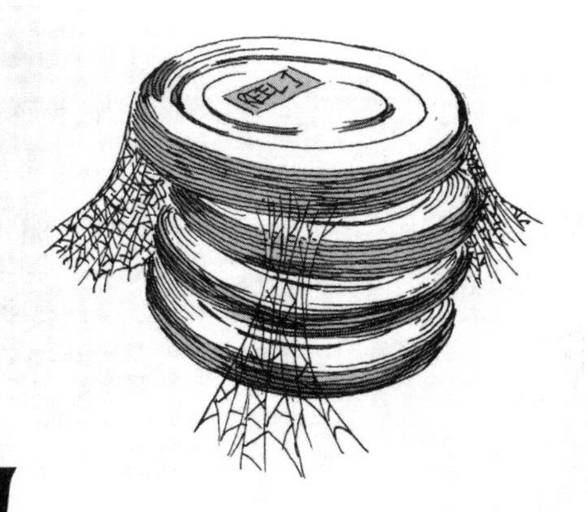

William was still staring into the searing eyes of the portrait as the tale concluded. The librarian looked up from the page. "Good to his word, the Count retired to our humble abode but insisted on continually transforming into a bat or a wolf, so we had to ask him to leave due to our strict 'no pets' policy. But he did not go far. He keeps to the yard, wandering the grounds and howling at the moon. His brethren, however, are still quite active in the community."

"I'm not interested in vampires. I only want to hear from . . ."

"A ghost?"

"My sister."

At that very moment, someone called his name. William turned with renewed hope. It was a voice he hadn't heard in years, except in old family videos and a phone message he clung to. Was it wishful thinking? Or a cheap trick, perpetrated by the librarian? The unbeliever in William assumed the latter. "That was low. Having a girl's voice call my name. It's about as low as . . ."

"Something *you* might have done?" The librarian seemed to know more about William than he was saying. "I assure you, there is no trickery involved."

"We'll see about that." William took off, sprinting down the corridor. "And don't try following me!"

William made his way into a large foyer, then began climbing a grand staircase. At the top, he began checking doors, jiggling knobs to the left and the right, before eventually making his way up another set of stairs, not knowing where they led. The attic, he hoped. **Does no one heed my warnings?**

The stairs themselves seemed to defy gravity, and William found himself running upside down, like a bug on the ceiling. His conclusion was that the mansion was an impossible feat of engineering. The only other option was that he had gone utterly insane. William chose to focus on the former.

He heard music, a funerary march, somewhere nearby. It was a tune the dead might dance to. But William wasn't about to stop. A lone door lay up ahead and William ran right through it. Had he gone the opposite way, he would have crossed a balcony overlooking a ballroom . . . where a party was in progress. A party attended by the dead. With the guest of honor . . .

His dearly departed sister.

The door flew open and William barreled through, stumbling headfirst over a stack of metal canisters. Right away, he knew what they were. Old movie reels. He had somehow found his way into the mansion's projection booth. ***Didn't see that on the tour, did you?***

William got to his feet, at the same time spotting a gaunt figure standing beside an antiquated movie projector. It was the librarian, who'd been expecting William just as surely as William had been expecting him. "Do you frequent the cinema, Master William?"

"What? No. Not anymore."

"But you used to . . . when you were a child."

"I used to see scary movies with my sister. But I'm not a kid anymore." William sighed. "Look, I don't know what your game is . . ."

"This is not a game." The librarian spun the movie reel. "I have something rare to show you."

"I thought you were a keeper of books."

"Of tales. And what is cinema but an extension of the written word? Although I do prefer parchment to celluloid."

The projector came to life, its take-up reel stubbornly pulling the film through its rusted gears.

"Arcane, I don't have time to watch a—"

The librarian pressed a bony finger to his lips. "Shhhh! Don't spoil it for the audience."

William was at his wits' end. "What audience?"

The librarian pointed to a rectangular slot, which overlooked an old theater. William took a peek down below. The seats were filled with patrons whose features William could not see in the dark. Nor would he have wanted to. They were residents of the mansion, no longer in the pink. But William did have an unobstructed view of the screen, where the opening moments of our next tale were flickering to life.

Chapter Eight

Have you seen any ghosts lately? I'll wager you have.

In fact, I know you have. The trick is knowing where to look. We begin, naturally, with the most obvious places: your attic, your basement, inside your closet, under your bed . . . You get the idea. These are all decent dwellings for a happy haunt to hide in. But the most likely place to find a ghost happens to be right on your TV, or in an old movie theater.

Many of the thespians appearing in old movies have since departed their corruptible mortal vessels, yet we still see and hear them today, as youthful and vibrant as they were in the past. They are ghosts, repeating their routines for all eternity, insisting we laugh or cry or scream until we faint.

So if you're really interested in seeing a ghost, try watching an old flicker—I mean, movie. One or two are bound to turn up.

Today's screaming—ahem, screening—involves a young man's undying love of film. Until he watches one spook show too many. So grab your popcorn and let's go to the movies.

Lights! Camera! Terror!

Uncle Rory's Late Show

The day Uncle Rory died was the second-worst day of Mark's life. The day Uncle Rory came back from the dead was the worst.

Interior, Uncle Rory's Bijou theater, night.

Uncle Rory clasped his hands like he was praying, but he wasn't. "You can't take her from me." He dropped to his knees. "Please, Mr. Trevelyn. She's all I have." It wasn't like Uncle Rory to beg. He was a proud man. But desperate times called for desperate measures. The creep from the bank had just delivered a death blow in the form of a foreclosure notice. Meaning that in thirty days' time, Uncle Rory's Bijou would be no more. Meaning it was time to beg. "Please. I'll do anything."

But Mr. Trevelyn wouldn't budge, which was why the bank had sent him in the first place. He was their hatchet man. A crusher of dreams. And Mr. Trevelyn loved his job. "On your feet, Mr. Subotsky. You're making a bloody fool of yourself."

Uncle Rory remained, knees on the carpet. "I'm willing to do that. I'll be your fool. I'll do whatever it takes to keep what's mine."

The banker found that last bonbon especially amusing. "You mean, what's ours."

"N-n-not the Bijou."

"Especially the Bijou. You have one month to vacate the premises. Is that clear, Mr. Subotsky?" He waited for a response, but none was forthcoming. Uncle Rory's chest had tightened and his breath was nearly gone. (There's a medical term for that, but let's just call it heartache.) You see, Uncle Rory had put everything he had into restoring the Bijou, a two-thousand-seat movie palace boasting one giant screen instead of twenty: a cathedral where the ghosts of

Hollywood's past could perform their antiqued rituals night after night, in flawless repetition.

"Answer the question, Mr. Subotsky. For legal purposes, do you understand the terms?"

Uncle Rory placed his finger to his lips. "Shhhhhhhh! No shouting during showtime. You'll ruin it for the audience."

"What audience?" Trevelyn chuckled. It sounded cruel, as the truth sometimes did. That night, the Bijou was playing host to an audience of one.

Mark was the audience's name. He had the balcony to himself, gleefully munching popcorn, engrossed in a black-and-white spook show he'd seen about thirty-two times. Mark adored old movies almost as much as he adored his uncle Rory, which was no coincidence. His uncle had introduced him to the magic of film in the first place: "the only real magic in a mostly unmagical world." And he proved it! With the flick of a projector switch, Mark could be transported to far-off lands, to 20,000 leagues under the sea or galaxies far, far away. To a world where singin' in the rain inspired tears of joy, as opposed to the kind that were currently flowing in the lobby.

Mark walked down from the balcony, grinning—"What an ending, what an ending!"—and spotted Uncle Rory, still on his knees, sobbing. "Unc, you okay?" Something awful must have happened. He hadn't seen his uncle cry since they'd colorized *It's a Wonderful Life.*

"It's over, Mark."

Mark helped him to his feet. "Yeah. It ended about a minute ago. Clean print, great sound."

"Not the movie—the Bijou."

"What are you talking about?"

"That Peter Lorre–looking character who was just here, he's from the bank." Uncle Rory held out the foreclosure notice and Mark turned away, refusing to see what was right in front of him. "Everyone said a movie palace was a bad move." Uncle Rory shook his head despairingly. "The kids won't come. They watch movies on their phones, if they watch 'em at all. Why didn't I listen?"

"I came!" Mark did his best to look cheery and even threw in a few steps from his happy dance.

Uncle Rory caressed his nephew's shoulder. "You see the box office? You're the only one who came. And you got in for free."

Wow. Uncle Rory was sounding more desperate than a sequel. **Or a volume two. Heh-heh.** True, it had been ages since the Bijou had enjoyed a packed house. Even the midnight spook show—a onetime guaranteed sellout—no longer drew a crowd. The untimely death of the central air conditioner, may it rest in peace, probably hadn't helped. But maybe it had to do with the movies themselves—golden oldies, as they're sometimes called, when the colors of the world appeared in black and white and movie stars looked like Clark Gable and Diana Durwin.

"Things will pick up," Mark promised, a white lie he hoped would come to pass. "Maybe Mom can dip into her retirement fund." But even Mark knew that was reaching. His mother only believed in things she could touch. The Bijou was a place for dreamers.

"It's not up to your mom. Maybe if we could get John Wayne to jump off the screen and vanquish the bad guys." He gave Mark a consolation squeeze before turning for the lights. "This is the end. Fade to black. Roll the credits."

Mark watched with a heavy heart as Uncle Rory threw the main switch, extinguishing the neon sign. On the street below, the Bijou marquee went dark.

The last spook show came that Saturday night, with Mark watching, misty-eyed, from the balcony as the ghosts of the Bijou took their final bow. A square-jawed hero had just obliterated a slimy gray creature, and the mad scientist's lab exploded into a mushroom cloud—all without the encumbrance of color. And when THE END zoomed out of the screen, it took on a whole new meaning. Mark almost broke down like his uncle had. There would be other movies, of course, in theaters the size of closets. But their special home, the Bijou, was riding off into the sunset.

When he bent down to get his empty popcorn bucket, the screen erupted with blinding light. Mark knew what it meant. The film had left the projector. Something wasn't right. Uncle Rory never allowed a movie to flicker past its final frame. Just as troubling: the house lights hadn't come up. Again, that was unlike Uncle Rory. The audience deserved better. Anything less was multiplex.

Mark flew down the stairs from the balcony, fearing the worst. If life *had* been a movie, the music would have been swelling to support a close-up on his running feet.

He circled the second-floor lobby, calling out his uncle's name. There was no response. He checked everywhere: the closet, the concession stand, both restrooms. Where had Uncle Rory gone? Then he spotted the red door to the holiest of holy sanctuaries: the projection booth.

Deeming it an emergency, Mark entered without knocking.

"Uncle Rory?" The projector was still running. He could hear the take-up reel spinning, loose film flapping. "Uncle Rory," he said again. And when he saw the body, he shouted it. *"Uncle Rory!"*

Mark's uncle was propped up next to the projector, his cheek pressed against the casing, feeling the final beats of its Bell and Howell heart. Uncle Rory's own ticker had sputtered to a stop just moments before, something the local coroner would later rule a massive coronary. But Mark knew better. He had seen enough movies to know.

Uncle Rory had died of a broken heart.

A month to the day after Uncle Rory's final death scene, Mark watched from a park bench as a wrecking ball completed the montage, reducing his happiest place on earth to a mound of rubble. The Bijou was . . . *gone with the wind.*

Later in the week, Mark joined his mother at a lawyer's office for the reading of Uncle Rory's will. Not particularly exciting events, such readings—just a room full of vultures waiting to hear their names called, hoping the dead guy left them something good. In Uncle Rory's case, after the Last National Bank got through with everything, very few assets remained. There sat Mr. Trevelyn, free of shackles, void of guilt. How many others had there been? How many dreams had this creep squashed?

Uncle Rory's lawyer got to the section of the will involving Mark. "'To my dear nephew, I bequeath the key to your dreams.'" The lawyer reached into an envelope and withdrew a cheap brass key, then slid it across the table to Mark.

Trevelyn couldn't help snickering. "Just your luck, kid. He left you a metaphor."

The lawyer cleared his throat. "If you'll allow me to continue." Reading on: "'The contents of unit 1939 located on Buena Vista Avenue are yours, dear nephew. Keep in mind . . . the audience demands a proper ending.'"

Mark smiled, hearing those words, his uncle's mantra. He was right, of course. Movies were all about the endings. Especially the golden oldies, in which the heroes always won and the villains were properly punished. Seated across from the banker, Mark could well imagine Mr. Trevelyn's ending, a juicy death scene in 3-D. He juggled the key between his hands. What did it unlock? **What dreams may come? Mark will find out soon enough. And if you consider "happily ever after" a proper ending, stop reading at once, foolish reader. Here at the mansion, we prefer "They all died miserably."**

—

CHAPTER EIGHT

That evening, Mark's mom had a big date, so he had to wait until the next day to explore unit 1939. **Really, now. Would *you* wait? I thought not. Neither would young Mark.**

Mark skateboarded to a dull-as-dirt industrial building on Buena Vista Avenue, arriving just before sunset. A black-and-white banner for Keep It Here Storage was fluttering in the wind. Mark entered through the customer service door. The reception desk was unmanned, but it did have a bell with a small sign that said to ring it. So Mark rang it. *Fourteen times.*

A figure backed in from the adjoining office, illuminated by a shaft of harsh light. It was an older woman wearing a fancy black evening gown. *A tad overdressed for Keep It Here Storage,* thought Mark. Before she turned, he tried guessing what she might look like. A prune, most likely. Which was okay. He liked prunes. But the last thing he expected was to see a face he recognized. True, she now sported wrinkles, and her famous blond tresses had turned gray, but her beauty, it was timeless. Even her skin retained an unnatural luminosity. It must've been the light, because the woman seemed literally to flicker. "May I help you?"

"I-I-I'm sorry," stammered Mark. "I didn't mean to stare. It's just . . . Can you tell me how to find unit 1939?"

"Of course, darling. That's why I'm here."

She delivered it like a line from an old movie. There could be no doubt. It *was* her, eighty years past her Hollywood prime. Mark knew the answer, but he asked anyway: "Didn't you used to be Diana Durwin?"

"'Used to be,'" the woman said with a whiff of disdain. "Have I been replaced?"

"No, never! You were—are—irreplaceable."

"You're too kind. And I'm very lucky. It's a gift to be recognized, especially by one so young."

He recognized her, all right. Diana Durwin had been one of Uncle Rory's absolute favorites, the Oscar-nominated star of *A Life Remembered.* "I used to watch you all the time at my uncle's theater."

"I know."

"You do? How?"

"I could see you from the screen."

A fun idea, he thought. *Movie stars watching the audience the way an audience watches them.* But Diana Durwin wasn't being coy. "Since the Bijou's demise," she went on, "my kind have been out of circulation. Oh, we occasionally show up on television. But so few tune in. We belong on the big screen, where the colors of the real world shall forever remain in black and white."

"Your kind?" asked Mark. "Who's your kind?"

"The ghosts of the silver screen."

"You were always the most beautiful," he added.

"And forever shall be . . . with your help." Diana Durwin turned to her best side, left profile, and the years seemed to vanish before Mark's startled eyes. He was seeing her as she had been, yesteryear's top starlet. "Do you believe in magic?" she asked. "The magic of the movies?"

"I—I always have."

Ms. Durwin nodded her approval. "Rory chose wisely."

"You knew my uncle?"

"He was our greatest benefactor, without whom our kind would be forgotten." She lifted her chin, striking a new pose, the cover of *Screen Daily*, circa 1939. "I was sent to find you, Mark."

"I don't understand. By who?"

"By your uncle, naturally. We made provisions. In case he, how shall I put it, departed this world suddenly. Oh, yes, arrangements were made. You did bring the key, didn't you?"

The key, yes! Unit 1939. Mark hadn't thought about its

significance before. That was a golden year for movies. *Gone with the Wind, The Wizard of Oz, Stagecoach, Son of Frankenstein.* He could go on.

"Don't forgot *Tainted Rose,*" added Diana Durwin.

"Uncle Rory's favorite!"

"He had excellent taste," opined the star of *Tainted Rose.* "It's showtime, Mark. Well begun is half done!" She gave him detailed directions to the unit. "And keep in mind: the audience demands a proper ending."

Mark started to leave, then lingered, staring a moment longer. How was it possible? Diana Durwin wouldn't be alive, and even if she were, she shouldn't be working at Keep It Here Storage.

Diana Durwin smiled at him and turned to walk in the opposite direction, slowly drifting out of the light. "You're a doll," she said as she disappeared down a seemingly endless corridor. Mark should have been beaming; this was better than an autograph. But he didn't feel happy. Instead, a chill rippled through him. Mark noticed something he hadn't before. The woman he had been speaking to was colorless. As she had been in her heyday . . .

Diana Durwin appeared in black and white.

Chapter Nine

Mark got lost twice before finding his way to unit 1939. From the outside, it looked like a regular roll-up door, protected by an old padlock. Mark took out the key, pausing before unlocking it. Uncle Rory's final gift was in that room. We've all opened presents, hoping for winners, coming up with underwear. What if this turned out to be just that? Perhaps not knowing would be better.

Who are we kidding? Mark undid the lock as fast as he could, whipped the door up to the ceiling, and clicked on the light. And for the love of all things Hollywood, his eyes almost fell out of his skull. ***But "almost" doesn't count, except in "I almost made it out in one piece."***

Unit 1939 was loaded with metal canisters, a veritable treasure trove for those who knew what they were. Mark knew. They were movies, hundreds of them, on actual film, not a digital pixel in sight. He tilted his head, practically drooling as he read some of the titles. *Hmmm,* London After Midnight. *That one sounds interesting.* A thousand hours of forgotten gems just waiting to be rediscovered. If only he had the projector to run them.

A flickering light appeared on the cinder block wall. Mark turned around, finding a vintage movie projector, immaculately maintained, facing the wall's makeshift screen. ***Their kind thought of everything.***

The projector grumbled with starvation; any film would do. Mark reached for the nearest reel, the one by his feet. He attached it to the spindle, feeding the celluloid strip into the belly of the projector. The proud device burped its approval. Sitting on a stack of canisters, Mark faced the wall, imagining he was back at the Bijou.

A black-and-white image appeared, the opening moments of a movie Mark had never seen.

It took place inside a coffin.

CHAPTER NINE

—

Crawling out of a grave is never easy. For starters, you have to make your way through an inch and a half of coffin. Even the cheap pine boxes prove arduous. But if you have revenge on your brain, even if your brain's turned to mush, you'll find a way. The undead always do.

The shadowed corpse inside the coffin *did* have revenge on its brain. A condescending chuckle—something the rotting corpse had heard before it died—echoed through its skull, enraging it, yet affording it a patience it hadn't known in life. Pressing its finger against the lid of the casket, the corpse began to scratch. And scratch and scratch and scratch.

It scratched until the nail fell off.

It scratched until the bone of its forefinger sharpened into a makeshift tool.

It scratched until a tiny hole formed in the lid, until an avalanche of mud forged a path through that hole, expanding the opening until the coffin imploded and the earth absorbed the corpse.

The first obstacle had been defeated. Yet the ground was cumbersome. Climbing through six feet of putrid muck would be an insurmountable task for the living. The dead, however, were another matter. They had time to kill. And the vengeful dead . . .

they had patience.

Mark switched off the projector, having seen too much. He loved a good spook show more than anyone, but this was different. This was real. It was the single most realistic film he had ever seen, its unforgettable images scorched into his thirteen-year-old gray matter along with other sensations. The sound of the grave, the smell of steaming hot flesh permeating from the celluloid. Normally, a film of such power would have Mark running off to sing its praises. That night, he ran off in terror. For the first time in his moviegoing life, Mark had seen a film he wanted to forget.

His mother was waiting on the porch when Mark skateboarded up the driveway. She sprang to her feet. "Where have you been?"

"The movies." Mark's brain was working overtime, trying to make him unsee what he had just seen. And having no luck.

"Why didn't you call?" But after noticing the look on his face, she took it down a notch. Uncle Rory's death had taken a toll on everyone. "All right, what did you see?"

"Nothing. Never mind. It was terrible." He started for the door.

She knew something was wrong. Mark always had time to dissect a movie, especially one he didn't like. She sat back down, patting the step to invite him to join her. Mark hesitated. "What?" he said. She patted it again and he gave in. His mom often had to play both parents, since his dad had pulled a reboot. This was one of those times. "What really happened today?" she asked.

"Do you believe in the magic of the movies?"

His mother smiled; Mark sure sounded like his old self. She thought about it. "I believe there are a handful of movies that are special, movies that have changed lives. Not the vast majority, mind you. But the special few. If that's magic, then yes, I guess I believe."

"Not like that. I'm talking about actual power, about real magic."

"What are you trying to say?"

"Forget it." He stood up, ready to go inside. That was when he saw his mother's expression. She was greatly disturbed, too. "You okay, Mom?"

"Not really." Tears began streaming down her cheeks. An unusual plot twist. His mom was not a crier.

"What happened? Tell me."

"I promised myself I wouldn't. With all you've been through lately . . ."

"Well, now you *have* to tell me!"

She wiped the tears from her face, straightening her posture. She had to look strong. The thing she had to tell him . . . it was monstrous. "I got a call a little while ago. From the Eternal Grace Cemetery."

Mark felt his insides drop. **Oh, such lovely images.** His mother continued: "It's . . . about Uncle Rory. I'm sure you guessed as much." She turned her head, for the moment unable to look his way. Then she uttered a sentence so unbelievable, just hearing it felt like a bad dream. "Someone dug up his grave." She stopped. Took a breath. "His coffin's empty. Uncle Rory's gone."

Less than an hour later, Mark was in his bedroom, pacing, Uncle Rory's words echoing in surround sound: *The audience demands a proper ending.* But it was impossible. Movies weren't real life. Or were they? Because by then he knew: Uncle Rory's corpse hadn't been stolen. As in the movie, it had clawed its way out of its grave! If part one had come true, and Mark had a feeling it had, then what terrors did the sequel have in store? To find out, Mark would have to go back to unit 1939 and watch the ending of the most terrifying movie ever made.

But before he left, Mark looked up Diana Durwin in *The Big Book of Movie Stars,* a gift from Uncle Rory. She was a star, all right. She had page 666 all to herself; her picture, credits, and awards were all there, along with some spine-tingling trivia. Diana Durwin had been blacklisted from Hollywood because of her alleged ties to witchcraft and the occult. *Perfect casting,* Mark thought.

Unit 1939 had already been unlocked by the time Mark got there. **They were expecting him.** He rolled up the metal door and entered to find the projector once again growling in hunger and anticipation. Mark fed it some film.

On the cinder block wall, a black-and-white world resolved into being: it was an establishing shot of a town Mark recognized—*his* town—only now it was mired in fog, as if it was the setting of an old-fashioned spook show. The landmarks looked different, because he'd only seen them in color before. Rosie's Ice Cream Shop and the gazebo where Mark almost got his first kiss. **But "almost" doesn't count, except** in *"I almost didn't fall off that cliff."* The location was Main Street, a scant few blocks from where he was now. A faint glow was coming from the office of the Last National Bank.

Mark could guess where the scene was going. It was only a matter of time before . . .

Scrunch! A lanky figure entered from the left of the screen. *Scrunch!* The sound of footsteps emerged from the speaker and the shot changed to a close-up of Uncle Rory's burial shoes, encrusted in mud. From there, the pictures kept coming. Uncle Rory's corpse was sauntering up the street, a mud trail in its wake. Here was a vision no makeup artist could ever achieve, nor would any want to. Uncle Rory, dirty, decomposing, and disgusting, was carrying a hatchet. Where he had found it was never explained. Movies are like that sometimes. But it wouldn't take a spoiler to know where he was headed. The corpse had an appointment with a banker.

The scene shifted to the banker's office. Mr. Trevelyn was at his desk, looking even creepier in monochrome. He was there late, finishing up some paperwork, cheerfully whistling as he placed a lien on the DeToth School for the Blind.

Kra-krak! A sound jerked him from his paperwork. *Krak!* The sound came again, and Trevelyn jumped out of his chair, holding his stapler defensively. "We're closed, whoever you are! Use the ATM!" But Uncle Rory wasn't there for money. *Krak!* The front door rattled. "I said we're closed!" Trevelyn yelled again. *KRRRAK!* The door split down the middle. Uncle Rory's hatchet was doing the work, coming down, going up, coming down, again and again!

Mark yelled at the screen, a habit he normally deplored. "Run, you dummy! Get out of there!" The film then cut to the hallway outside Trevelyn's office. The corpse turned briefly, pressing a finger to its scabbed lips. "Shhhhhhh." Mark's blood went cold. The corpse could see him through the screen!

Back inside the office, Mr. Trevelyn slid away from his desk and fell over his chair, but it was too late. The corpse was in the room, and its rotting form was already standing over the banker's body. Trevelyn could see its grisly countenance. He looked away, but it was no use. Flecks of decaying flesh peeling from the bone were reflected in the floor. Trevelyn slowly turned to face the corpse and immediately recognized the vengeful features that had survived the grave. "No! Not you! It *can't* be you!" Trevelyn looked and sounded more frightened than all the victims of Mark's favorite spook shows combined. Death had come for the banker, at twenty-four frames per second.

Uncle Rory's hatchet went up. . . .

Mark covered his eyes, something he never, ever did during a spook show. Why miss the good parts? But this movie was too realistic even for him to bear. So he shielded his eyes, forgetting about the sounds, which were far worse. Mark heard Trevelyn shouting at his uncle, continuing to insult him as he had done when Uncle Rory was alive. But Trevelyn did not beg, nor did he plead, as Uncle Rory had pleaded. He continued to be a first-class jerk right until his very last second, when, finally, he let out a scream that tested the limits of the old Bell and Howell speaker.

Next there was a *THUNK!* followed by precipitous silence. Even the music stopped, as if the banker *and* the orchestra had been cut off mid-octave.

Mark considered running off but knew it would be futile. You can't outrun a horror movie. The best ones find you wherever you are, at home, in bed, or even in a storage unit. So he lowered his hands and saw what came next. Uncle Rory's corpse was shuffling out the doorway of the Last National Bank, the suit they had buried him in splattered with what looked like chocolate syrup. He was no longer holding the hatchet. A different prop was clutched in his fist. At first, Mark couldn't make out what it was. Then, as if on cue, Uncle Rory lifted it so the camera could get a close-up.

Mark fell off the canisters when he saw it. The image was indelible, one he would never forget: Uncle Rory was carrying Mr. Trevelyn's head.

Mark's mom was watching the news when he burst into the den, ranting about a movie he'd just seen. She tried calming him down, but when he unloaded the details, she turned ashen. She'd just seen the same details on TV. The bank's hatchet man had been murdered **(by hatchet, heh-heh)** for real. The police were still looking for the fiend responsible.

"It was Uncle Rory!" shouted Mark, shaking uncontrollably. His mother pulled him in close for a hug.

"Hold it together, Mark, and start from the beginning."

"It's better if I show you."

"Show me? How? What are you talking about?"

Mark held up the key. "I'm talking about unit 1939."

The car ride to Buena Vista Avenue took less than five minutes, with Mark filling in all the lurid details, which his mother had a hard time swallowing. Such things only happened in, well . . . in the movies. **Or a haunted mansion.**

Bypassing the reception area, they went straight to the unit. The roll-up door looked different—forest green instead of black—and the lock was missing. "Somebody stole the lock," Mark explained to his mother. Not one to waste time, she grabbed the handle and yanked open the door. And after her initial survey . . .

"Well?"

Mark stepped in beside her and gasped. It was shocking. The unit had been cleared out: the canisters, the projector—all gone. "This place was packed an hour ago. Mom, I swear it! The films were stacked this high." He approximated their height with his hand. "The projector was plugged in over there!" He pointed to the wall. But all his mother saw was an uncomfortably large spiderweb. There was no projector, not even an outlet.

"Mark, I know you're having a rough time, what with Uncle Rory's passing . . ."

Mark was so frustrated his head almost exploded. **But almost doesn't cou—Never mind.** "I'm not crazy!" He grabbed her hand. "Come with me. Right now! I need you to meet someone."

He dragged his mother down the main stairwell, emerging into the reception area on level one. This time, there wasn't an aged starlet behind the desk. There was an old man playing solitaire with—get this—actual cards. Right away, Mark demanded to know what had happened to the woman.

"What woman?"

"The one who works here!"

The old man shook his head. "Just me, son. And has been for goin' on twenty-two years." He played his next card, the queen of hearts, and smiled.

Mark's mother took over. "My son was just here. He says unit 1939 was loaded and now it's empty."

The old man lost his smile and Mark instantly knew why. Unit 1939 scared him. "That's n-n-not possible," stammered the old man. "Unit 1939 has been off limits for years."

"Why?" demanded Mark.

"You don't want to know why, son. Now if there's nothing else I can do for you . . ." He pretended to continue his game.

"Why are you afraid to tell us? Please, sir, I need to know. What happened up there?"

The old man didn't want to talk about it. These days, he didn't even want to think about it. But there was such desperation in Mark's voice, he decided he had to. "There was trouble up there, a bunch o' years back. A movie star was livin' in the unit. She couldn't afford to live nowhere else. Sad case. She was pretty old at the time. About as old as I am now. And forgotten. It only came to our attention when the other customers started complainin'."

"Complaining about what?"

"The stink. Oh, and the maggots. There's always those." Mark trembled, and suddenly, the old man was more than happy to share the details, as if they were the finale to his creepy campfire story. "She died up there, all alone. And her body started to rot." The old man snapped his fingers, trying to recall. "What was her name? Famous one day, forgotten the next."

But Mark remembered. She had been his uncle's favorite when the Bijou was alive. "Diana Durwin," he said. The old man nodded. "And thanks to Uncle Rory, she will never be forgotten."

At the mention of the name, the old man looked up at Mark and his mom. "You knew Rory?"

"Yes, he was my uncle," Mark replied as his mother put a steadying hand on his shoulder.

"Of course. You're the nephew. I should've known," the

old man said as he reached under the desk. "Rory left you something."

"I know," said Mark. "He left me the key to unit 1939."

"He left you something a lot more valuable than that." The old man handed Mark a metal film canister.

That night, Mark carefully threaded the film into his uncle's old projector. He had convinced his mother to let him watch it first, by himself, with the lights out, just as Uncle Rory would've wanted.

The projector flickered to life. Once again, it was a black-and-white film that looked just a little too realistic. The camera glided silently through the familiar streets, passing the gazebo, passing Rosie's Ice Cream Shop. Mark felt a swell of anticipation, because he knew where the shot was headed. And he was not wrong. The camera settled on a wide-angle view of Uncle Rory's Bijou. The grand old movie palace was back in all its past splendor. The marquee was shining and there was a line of patrons rounding the block, waiting to pile in for the midnight spook show.

The movie continued, the camera moving through the town. A dissolve soon gave way to the Eternal Grace Cemetery, and Mark heard a quiet shuffling sound emerge from the speaker. It grew louder and louder until, finally, the star of the show made his appearance. Uncle Rory had entered the frame, still holding the head of Mr. Trevelyn. A stunning woman in an evening gown greeted him at the entrance; it was Diana Durwin, looking as she had in 1939. She took Trevelyn's disembodied head, turned, and handed it to a ghostly figure that had emerged from a mausoleum. The strange apparition held a cane and wore a top hat and a cloak with a high pointed collar. He took the banker's head and placed it into a large container—***a hatbox, if you will***—then led them up the hill toward a grand old mansion. Uncle Rory, still deceased, thank you, but now looking a bit more like his old self, took Diana's arm and began to walk up the hill. But before reaching the top, he stopped and slowly turned to look directly into the camera—directly at Mark.

"The audience demands a proper ending," he said. Then the corpse of Uncle Rory winked, and with that, Mark turned off the projector just as the scene . . .

faded to black.

Chapter Ten

William left the projection booth in a hurry, but not before giving the movie a big thumbs-down. *(Everybody's a bloody critic.)* He discovered another staircase and, not heeding the librarian's warning *(because no one ever does)*, found his way into the attic.

The attic extended across the entire length of the roof, as its domed ceiling suggested. It was chilly during the winter months, strangely chillier in the summer. It housed an unusual assortment of mementos, just like *your* attic. Old lamps hung from supports, where spiders made their homes. There were mirrors and vanities and old chests, containing who knows what, along with an accumulation of forgotten wedding gifts. But what fascinated William the most were the portraits.

Wedding portraits, lined up against the wall, each featuring the same bride posed alongside a different groom. As William moved from painting to painting, the grooms' heads momentarily disappeared. Passing the last one, he saw a statuesque figure in the corner. A woman, dressed in white, with her back turned. It was the bride, preparing to walk down the aisle. Once again.

Not knowing who she was, William inquired: "Excuse me. Can you tell me about Madame Leota?"

The bride spun around, her feet never touching the floor. "Leota is dead!" she hissed, floating toward William, her face obstructed by a veil. "*I'm* the one you want!"

William was frozen, mesmerized by her ethereal presence. The bride moved closer. "We'll live happily ever after, till death do us part." She had something in her hands, but it wasn't a bouquet. The bride was holding a bloody ax, the fate of her suitors as obvious as her identity. She was Constance, the black widow bride, famous for lopping off her husbands' heads after procuring their wealth. *"Here comes the bride,"* she sang. "As long as we both shall live. For better or for worse. I do . . . I did."

She raised the ax. "In sickness and in wealth. You may now kiss the bride." Her veil lifted on its own and William screamed in a way he hadn't since he was a boy. He was looking into the eyeless sockets of a skeleton.

The sight jolted William back, sent him rolling over a trunk that contained her dowry. The ax slammed down, shredding the trunk, and William felt a breeze as the blade missed his throat by mere inches. He scrambled to his feet, knocking over furniture.

The bride kept coming at him, determined to have it her way. This time, she would get it right.

William made his way back to the stairs, or at least where he remembered the stairs had been. In their place, an impish little fellow with a paintbrush was adding the finishing touches to a new portrait. It featured the bride with her latest suitor—William himself!—minus his head. The grooms in the other portraits were chanting: "I do! I do! I do!" William covered his ears to prevent madness from creeping in. There was no way out! The bride had him cornered; she was levitating directly above him. A wedding would take place, with or without his permission. Followed by a beheading.

"Say 'I do.' It'll be over fast. Close your eyes. We weren't meant to last." William closed his eyes, the dutiful suitor, as the ax went up. But as he awaited the final blow . . .

a child's hand took hold of his, and William felt himself being whisked out of the attic. His eyes remain closed, and it felt like he was flying, the way he used to in his dreams. It was only a few seconds before he touched down, not knowing where he had landed but grateful to be alive.

William opened his eyes, half expecting to find himself home in bed, still a kid, having dreamed his entire adult life. That was not the case. He was still in the mansion, still an adult, holding hands with the tiny stranger who'd saved his hide. "Thank you." The girl clasping his hand did not answer. She was no more than twelve; her frail frame suggested she was even younger.

"Who are you?" he asked. "What's your name?" She peered into William's eyes. Hers were the palest, saddest eyes he'd ever seen. She wore a flowered sundress and stood barefoot. "Where are your parents?"

"She does not speak," boomed a voice within the shadows. William turned, knowing who it was. "Arcane!" The librarian inched his way out of the darkness, his candlestick introducing light to the room. They were back in the library. "How did I get here?"

"You never left," replied the librarian.

"That's ridiculous. I just came from the attic. There's a woman up there, a crazy lady with an ax!"

"Yes, that would be Constance," replied the librarian. "I *did* warn you not to go up there."

William continued to rant. "I barely made it out alive! I wouldn't have, if it hadn't been for her." He gestured toward the girl, who remained silent.

"Ah, yes. Mistress Camille," the librarian said. He smiled and gave the girl a reassuring nod.

"What about her? Why is she here?"

"Because she chooses to be."

William felt a sudden and overwhelming need to protect her. "I don't believe you. Have you been keeping her here?" He made a beeline for the librarian, getting directly in his face.

This confounded the librarian. "Master William, we don't keep anyone . . . against their will." He beckoned the girl to his side, gently stroking her hair. "Mistress Camille may come and go as she pleases." The librarian plucked something from her hair. It was a live cockroach.

William needed to understand. This was no longer about him. Or Madame Leota. Or his sister. "All right, let's go. What's her story?"

"I thought you'd never ask." The librarian raised his candlestick and returned to his chair, where volume two was waiting. The time had come for William to receive his final lesson . . . in death.

Chapter Eleven

What is it about bedrooms? Your bedroom, in particular? It has everything you could ever want. Your TV, your clothes, your favorite games and knickknacks. All chosen by you, for you . . . except for that rug your mom insisted on.

It even has a night-light, just in case.

When you think about it, it's the safest room in the house. Until the lights go out. Because that's when *they* come. They mostly hide in closets and under beds. You'll hear a sound behind your wall and think, I'm being *silly*. It feels especially silly when the sun is up. But in the dark, when the hairs on the back of your neck are standing on end, you'll know . . . everything is *not* going to be all right.

So pull the covers over your head. It's safer that way.

Think good thoughts. That helps, too.

And know for certain that on any one of those nights, that visitor in your closet or the thing under your bed might yank those covers from your eyes. And in that moment, you'll realize you weren't being silly. You'll understand that your room is their room, too.

It happens more often than you think. It happened to Camille. It could happen to you.

Tonight.

The Roaches

Unspeakable acts had happened in the house where Camille had come to stay.

In 1865, the year Halloway House was born, a woman named Missy Cooledge chopped her husband into pieces with a meat cleaver and hid his body parts inside a cord of wood. In 1902, the Swanson family resided there for less than a fortnight before fleeing the house in terror, claiming it was possessed by demonic forces. Perhaps the most widely reported incident occurred in 1931. The writer Jerome Selby, famous for his historical opus, *We Weep for Thee,* had sublet a room for the summer, as he was preparing a gothic novel about the ghosts of Maine. On the morning of July 21, a servant discovered Selby's body hanging from a ceiling fan, his unfinished novel still on the nightstand, a single sentence scribbled across all 249 pages: *They come in through the walls.*

As circumstance secured its sinister reputation, Halloway House became a favored destination of paranormal investigators and the morbidly curious. Prominent neighbors petitioned to have it demolished. Mired in red tape, the request withered; in 1955 the Cortland family of New York City purchased the land and had Halloway House declared a historic landmark, permanently thwarting the wrecking ball. In September of the following year, Halloway House opened its doors to the public, now as a bed-and-breakfast.

Since that time, the house has remained relatively sedate, barring a minor event in 1963, when a chandelier fell, injuring three guests in the lobby. Lawsuits were settled out of court and Halloway House endured. It is reasonable to suggest that over the course of centuries, bad things happen everywhere. It is the law of averages. So the old Victorian overlooking the crashing coastline of the Atlantic some fourteen miles north of Kennebunkport remains a popular destination today.

It was a month before the start of the new season

when Camille arrived with her aunt. She had never heard of Halloway House and therefore knew nothing of its reputation. Her aunt Rue had served as senior housemaid for twenty seasons before "inheriting" Camille the way one inherits fine china. By then, in her mid-fifties, Aunt Rue had a reputation for being a stern taskmaster. She had never married and her interest in children had long since waned. But as a proponent of discipline and hard work, she believed she would have made a most excellent parent.

Camille believed otherwise. She was the thirteen-year-old daughter of Aunt Rue's sister, Florence, who had died five years earlier. In a straitjacket. The recent death of Camille's father had given Aunt Rue legal guardianship of her niece. To those looking in, the arrangement appeared mutually beneficial. Camille was spared the orphanage, and Aunt Rue inherited a sizable monthly allowance. As one would imagine, Camille had become withdrawn and sullen. But there was an inner light behind those sad gray eyes. Some people are born good. Just as some houses are born bad. Aunt Rue saw it a different way.

"You're as undisciplined as a storm! And just as dumb." Aunt Rue's words were cruel but also literal. Camille hadn't spoken since the day her mother died. A specialist had labeled her a "selective mute," suggesting that Camille was silent by choice. She no longer had a reason to talk. Or sing. Or even scream. Aunt Rue had little sympathy. Life was hard on everyone. Including her. Especially her. "Get over it!"

During the car ride up, Aunt Rue outlined a list of chores, which she considered modest. "Your first day will be light. After settling in, you'll start in the lobby. The floors need to be buffed and polished. Are you hearing me?"

Camille was staring out the car window, watching the trees go by. Fruit was blossoming, the colors coming back. Her father would have commented on the view.

"Camille!" Camille looked left, where the view was decidedly worse. Aunt Rue had the face of a bitter old crone, with cold, pitiless eyes. "The doctors say you're a fake. I say you always have been. You had your parents fooled, your daddy mostly. But I know what you really are. Ugly things come in pretty packages. You're ugly, Camille. And now I've got you. By heavens, we've got each other!"

Camille gave no expression, turning back to her view of the trees. Her insides were numb. Too numb to laugh or to cry or to scream. Aunt Rue thought of her "fake" affliction another way. *She's trying to drive me mad, this devil with an angel's face. Sizing me up for a straitjacket, just like she did my sister!*

The car turned onto a private road lined with pear and apple trees that led to Halloway House. Yes, Camille was thinking, her father would have loved it there.

Halloway House was still vacant when they arrived. The staff wouldn't be returning for another week. The house itself was a handsome Victorian with vaulted ceilings and cozy brick fireplaces, featuring twenty-one bedrooms of varying sizes. The facilities were state-of-the-art for their time, a time when cell phones and the Internet were just the musings of science fiction. Despite its age, Halloway House was consistently ranked in the top twenty bed-and-breakfasts of North America.

Aunt Rue escorted Camille up the lobby stairs, proudly boasting of Halloway's notable guests: two vice presidents, a slew of famous writers, and even an old movie star, Diana Durwin. But she made no mention of its notable horrors.

Room six would be Camille's for the week. Aunt Rue unlocked the door and walked her inside. It was the most luxurious bedroom Camille had ever seen. The furnishings were gold-trimmed, the wallpaper gold-striped; there was even a canopy bed perpendicular to the south wall, the kind of bed she had once dreamed of, back when frivolous dreams seemed to matter. Aunt Rue remained in the doorway. "Do we approve?" Camille nodded. "Very well. Unpack your things. I'll be back to collect you in ten minutes." She moved off, the clumping of her shoes echoing throughout the empty corridor.

Camille quickly unpacked, hanging her meager belongings in a closet that could have accommodated five times the amount. The last item in her case was a journal, which she hadn't written in since her father's death. She placed it on the vanity by the window. She needed to write again. For her own sanity, Camille needed to talk to someone, even if it was herself. She picked up a pen and opened her journal. Camille flipped through the book, in search of a blank page in which to write her new entry. But something stopped her: it was her last entry.

Camille's last recorded entry was on a Friday—*Daddy bringing home surprise*—the day of the accident. The black ink had been spattered with tears. How many times had she cried on that page, trying to recapture the feeling she had when she wrote it? The past felt like a dream—*Mommy and Daddy are alive.*

No, they're not. Wake up, Camille, you're dreaming!

Camille dropped her pen, partly because the words weren't coming, but mostly because of the sounds. She heard a noise she didn't recognize coming from behind the bed. For most, it would have been too faint to hear, but losing the ability to speak had served to heighten her other senses. Camille heard *everything.*

It was coming from behind the wall.

She tiptoed over and pressed her ear against the striped wallpaper. By then, the sounds were already starting to wane. They weren't coming from the pipes, Camille decided, or the furnace powering up. They were deliberate. Something was alive back there. Alive and on the move.

A loud, disciplined knock interrupted her. Camille looked at her watch. Ten minutes had passed, to the second, and Aunt Rue had returned to collect her niece. "It's time to earn your keep."

That afternoon, Aunt Rue went into town for supplies, leaving Camille to explore the property on her own. The grounds were idyllic. There were fruit trees and sloping hills and a freshwater stream where Camille skipped stones. It was like living in a painting.

Except for the flowers.

Exotic varieties from all over the world lined the perimeter of the estate. Beautiful to look at but deadly in their implications. Camille suffered from severe allergies; all insects posed a threat, and the flowers were overrun by bees. For Camille, the encompassing blooms were like an electrified fence. Any attempt to escape Halloway House could prove fatal.

Dinner took place in the main dining room, which could accommodate fifty guests. That night, there was seating for two: Camille and Aunt Rue. The meal was liver and steamed vegetables. The jellylike main course made Camille sick to her stomach. She slid the plate away and motioned to be excused. Aunt Rue didn't acknowledge her until Camille got to her feet.

"Where do you think you're going?"

Camille pointed: *upstairs.*

"Not before finishing every last morsel on that plate." Camille shook her head and started for the lobby. As she passed, Aunt Rue popped up from her chair and snatched

Camille by the bicep. "Just so we're clear: I talk, you listen. I believe that is the arrangement you've insisted upon. You lost a father and I lost a sister. For the time being, we're stuck with each other. There isn't much I can do about that. In less than a week, the first guests arrive. I have a job to uphold, which is seeing to the needs of Halloway House while, in accordance with your mother's wishes, looking after you. Guess which job I prefer?"

Camille flared her nostrils. If she could have raged, screamed, shouted, she would have done so, but she could not. Aunt Rue had won the round. "I'll have your dinner sent up to your room. Set your alarm for five. We have a full day ahead."

Camille had made it halfway across the lobby before Aunt Rue called out again. "Cammie, dear!" Camille paused, not turning. "I'm surprised at you. Aren't you going to say good night?" Camille didn't need to look back. She knew with certainty . . . Aunt Rue was smiling.

It was after ten o'clock when Camille scribbled her first journal entry in months. She wrote: *I hate liver.* Then, after careful consideration, she altered it to say: *I hate Aunt Rue.* She closed her journal and contemplated her next move. The odor coming from her untouched dinner might have cinched it. She had to get away, to escape Halloway House before Aunt Rue cost Camille her sanity. Or before one of them was dead.

She climbed onto the canopy bed and lay on her side. The mattress was *heaven-ness,* a thought that made her smile. *Is that even a word?* It was to Camille. She only said words in her head, so there was no one to correct her. She reached for the nightstand and switched off the light. No small irony, Halloway House provided Camille with the best sleep she'd had in months.

It was 3:33 in the morning when all that changed.

Camille suddenly found herself trapped in a dark, dank space; she couldn't tell where. She kicked and clawed and cried out for help, and only then did she realize she was dreaming, because Camille wasn't mute in her dreams. But her voice was stifled by a different sound. Something nonhuman was approaching, building like a tsunami, a chirping sound emerging from the walls!

Camille's eyes popped open. She was panting as she looked about the room, unsettled by the unfamiliar surroundings. It all came flooding back. *Halloway House. Aunt Rue. Mommy and Daddy are dead.* But the strange sounds, those clarion chirps, were still in the room, rising to an almost deafening refrain.

Camille clicked on the lamp and held it to the wall. The wallpaper was rippling. Tiny shapes, numbering in the thousands, were migrating underneath; they were lined up in military precision, chirping as they traveled. Camille opened her mouth to scream but could barely manufacture a hiss. Out of some mad instinct, she kicked at the wall, tearing a hole in the wallpaper.

Then, suddenly, the chirping ceased, and for the moment, Camille questioned her own state of mind. Was the sound an extension of her dream?

The answer arrived when a waterfall of black cockroaches tumbled out of the breach like living plumbs, bouncing onto the bed, their numbers inexhaustible. Camille kicked and slapped, her voiceless mouth twisted with anguish. She leaped out of the bed and backed into the dresser, watching them swarm into the room. Reaching back in the dark, her hand found the dinner tray and squished into something moist and animated. Camille turned to look.

The liver was covered in roaches.

Her mouth formed a silent cry as she stumbled to the door. It flew open before she got there, slamming into her shoulder and throwing her facedown into a carpet of roaches. If there was a scream left inside her, that would have been the time to use it.

Aunt Rue flicked on the light and the roaches scattered, retreating under furniture and back inside the walls. She looked down condescendingly from the open doorway. "Why are you on the floor when you have a perfectly good bed to sleep in?"

Camille sat up, flustered, trying to breathe. To form words. Aunt Rue handed her a pen and pad from the night-stand. "You have something to contribute? Here. Write it for me."

Camille jotted a single word. When she handed it back, Aunt Rue read it aloud. "'Roaches.'" Camille nodded. "Where?"

Camille scribbled a bloodcurdling response: *They come in through the walls.*

Aunt Rue gave an impatient sigh. "Well, they're gone now. Roaches, if that's what they were, only come out in the dark. Might I suggest sleeping with the light on?"

Camille scribbled another sentence—*Won't stay room 6*—eliciting a laugh from Aunt Rue. "I'll have you know, room six is a privilege. We have guests booking a year in advance."

Not safe, read Camille's next note. Aunt Rue was incensed. "That's absurd! Of course it's safe." Camille pounded the dresser, knocking over an antique figurine. "Watch that temper, Camille. Or I'll have you sent to Shepperton—to the same sanitarium your mother died in—where you belong!"

Aunt Rue turned toward the corridor. Camille followed her out, sticking a final note into her hand. The one-word declaration seemed to resonate with Aunt Rue. It read: *Inheritance.* She crumpled the note into a ball. So the pathetic little mute knew how to fight when she had to. "There will be an exterminator on the premises first thing in the morning. Until then, there's a cot in the fruit cellar. You'll sleep down there for the remainder of your stay. In fact, it rather suits you." She pocketed the crumpled note and briskly moved off, leaving Camille to gather her things.

From within shadowy hiding spaces under the bed, an army watched her pack.

Camille found the fruit cellar on her own, the label being a complete misnomer, since it contained no fruit. It was more like a repair shop. The air was dank. Three sputtering bulbs suspended from beams provided what little light there was. Strewn across the concrete floor were ten partially assembled bar stools, a table with three missing legs, numerous light fixtures, cases of ceramic bath tiles, and lamp shades. Camille found a stained cot shoved between two chunky TVs. It was folded in half and looked as hard as a rock, with a steel support bar that would feel like a knife in her back, the opposite of the luxury mattress in room six. Still, it was better than sharing a bed with roaches.

Camille rolled the cot away from the wall and found an old towel to cover her feet. Awaiting sleep, she listened to the creaks and dripping sounds that old houses made so well. And when sleep finally came, she dreamed once more.

This time of roaches.

In the morning, Halloway House was alive with activity: footsteps and ringing telephones and the sound of handcarts rolling supplies off trucks as the regular staff checked in. Camille remained in the cellar, hearing the commotion but not seeing a soul, which suited her just fine. In her silent state, it was difficult being around new people. And Aunt Rue saw to it that she had more work than she could handle. Being handy with a needle and thread, Camille got the job of tailoring the staff uniforms, a task that would take her well into the wee hours of the next morning.

It was after three a.m. when Camille decided to call it

quits for the day. Her eyes were seeing double, and in the previous half hour, her mistakes had been piling up. She hung the last uniform on a pipe and wheeled out the cot. Sleep was going to feel so good. *Heaven-ness* was the word. In truth, Camille was so exhausted she could have slept on a bed of nails.

She clicked the main switch, extinguishing the trio of overhead lightbulbs. The fruit cellar went black, except for the three glowing balls lingering in her eyes. Soon they would be gone, too. Camille waved her hand in front of her face. Nothing. Not a thing, even an inch in front of her. She turned on her side and closed her eyes. If she could keep herself from thinking, sleep would come. And it did.

It took forty minutes for the terror to follow.

Camille's eyes popped open, unable to adjust because there was nothing to see. The fruit cellar was a black abyss, but she could still hear. Camille heard what sounded like raindrops pitter-pattering across the cement floor. She felt a presence down there with her. She sat up, mouth open, tasting the floating dust particles clinging to the humidity. Was that all it was?

No.

Something else was in the fruit cellar. She reached under

the cot and found her flashlight. Camille's knuckles brushed against what felt like pebbles. She wriggled her hand and the pebbles shifted. Camille knew what it meant. The ground was alive. Room six had been fumigated the previous morning, and the roaches needed somewhere to go. And the best place to go was down, down into the cellar.

She felt one creeping up her arm and flicked it away with the flashlight, then switched the flashlight on. A circle of light appeared on the wall. And within that circle, Camille saw what looked like dollops of black raindrops streaming down, then scattering in all directions. *Breathe,* Camille thought. *It's going to be all right. For heaven's sake, breathe!*

She tilted the flashlight, directing its beam to the ground. The floor was in motion, an ocean of roaches, their stampeding legs emulating the sound of a retreating storm as they withdrew from the light. Camille opened her mouth in what looked like a scream. *Push!* Camille thought. *It's in there! Scream! Scream!*

Nothing.

By then, the roaches had discovered the cot, something new to climb. Camille stood up and centered her feet, the left on top of the right, in the middle of the mattress, watching in horror as the little black monsters began their vertical climb up the metal legs, on a path to her toes. She redirected the light, hitting the leaders dead on, and something unexpected happened. The roaches held their position, avoiding the beam like it was a force field they could not cross. Aunt Rue said they only came out in the dark. If Camille could get to the light switch, which was a mere ten feet from the cot, maybe they'd retreat and go back to where they had come from. She had no choice but to try.

Camille knelt at the edge of the mattress, leveling the beam on the ground. Repelled by the light, the roaches scattered, clearing a path for her to follow. This was her chance. She set her feet on the cold hard ground and, with the flashlight trembling, slowly walked the trail, the roaches lining up on both sides of the beam, wiggling their antennae, watching, waiting for a single mistake so they could pounce. They must have numbered in the millions.

Camille made it to the switch as the roaches poured in behind her ankles. *Click!* The three overhead lights came on, and the roaches dispersed, scattering under furniture and into crevices. Camille watched them retreat for what felt like hours, when in reality it took only seconds. Soon the cellar floor was as it had been before they came. But returning to the cot was no longer a consideration. Camille needed to get out of the cellar; she'd sleep outside if she had to.

She made her way to a wooden staircase, fighting not to think about what would happen if the roaches got used to the light. Climbing two steps at a time, she reached the sunken trapdoor that would release her into the yard. Frantically, she pushed and pushed on the door. It was locked. And in that moment, Camille surmised the terrible truth—a truth too horrible yet somehow certain. Aunt Rue had locked her in from the outside.

Camille pounded at the wood slats with the flashlight, pounded until the flashlight broke to pieces. If only she could muster a scream. One good one ought to do it. *Hisssssss* was all she had.

She sat on the top step, rocking back and forth. *Think, think, think.* It would be dawn soon. Morning. Sunlight. She wouldn't have long to wait. Surely someone would check on the pathetic little mute in the fruit cellar. If not for Camille's sake, then for the sake of the uniforms she'd spent all night mending. All she had to do was wait it out. *Remember to breathe.*

Except . . . Except . . .

She actually saw it happen. The first hanging light, the one farthest away, flickered and died. Then came the stampede. The roach army was on the move again, holding position where the light ended. She had two lights remaining. But if they died, too . . .

Camille held vigil from the top step. The roach army did not move, and neither did she. Another twenty minutes passed before . . . before the next bulb, the one in the middle, went out. Once again, the roaches advanced, stopping just shy of the third and final circle of light, waiting patiently for their invitation to the dance.

Camille could not wait. She had to make it to the other side of the fruit cellar, where she'd seen a dumbwaiter in the wall, leading up to the kitchen. It was her best hope of escape.

Slowly she descended, one creaky step at a time. And just as she reached the middle of the stairs, the last bulb flickered out, shrouding the cellar in darkness. Camille's foot missed the next step and she lost her balance, teetering, trying to hold on. She fell forward, tumbling and twisting down the stairs, before landing with a thud on the hard floor.

Camille was out cold. Alone. In the dark. From within the abyss, the chirping army approached.

When she finally came to, Camille felt a tingling sensation all over her body. She was covered, head to toe, with roaches. She opened her mouth and, for the first time in years, unleashed a bellowing scream. It was like sounding the dinner bell. Camille finally had an uncontested reason to use her voice again, so she screamed. She screamed for all to hear. She screamed and screamed again until all of Halloway House rattled. And as she let out her last scream, as if in response from Aunt Rue—and from the house itself—the roaches piled in.

It was later deemed an accident. There was no evidence of foul play. No evidence of a locked trapdoor. No evidence of roaches. The pathetic little mute girl must have slipped and fallen. It was the law of averages. Bad things happened everywhere, even at Halloway House.

Especially at Halloway House.

The old Victorian overlooking the crashing coastline of the Atlantic some fourteen miles north of Kennebunkport remains a popular destination today, despite the reports of people hearing screams coming from the cellar. Despite the rustling in the walls.

Despite the roaches.

Chapter Twelve

The librarian closed his book, the last story completed. William turned to comfort the girl, but she was gone. "Camille. Where is she?"

"Why do you care? She's merely a character in a story. Isn't that right, Master William? Just like the others."

William shook his head. "She was real. I felt her. I still can! What have you done with her?"

"Merely preserved her tale for generations to come."

"What kind of a show are you running here, Arcane?"

"No show, Master William. Only tell." He pointed to

his books. "When the time comes, I would be delighted to share your tale."

William shook his head. "And you? Is *your* story up there on one of these shelves, Mr. Arcane?"

The librarian unleashed an especially toothy grin. "Mine, I'm afraid, is a tale for another day."

The librarian released the book, like one might release a dove, and William watched as it floated back to its space on the shelf. "How did you do that?"

"You studied magic. Perhaps you can tell me."

"I can't." William rotated, trying to take it all in. "I can't explain any of this."

That pleased the librarian. "The world is unexplainable. We're surrounded by the strange. The unknown. The often unimaginable. Yet you have deprived yourself of these wonders by choosing not to believe."

"As a kid, I believed in everything." His lip began to quiver. He might have cried had he not renounced the luxury. "It got taken from me. The magic. All of it. The same day she got taken."

"Most unfortunate. It appears I have wasted your time."

The bookshelf parted. It was time for William to leave.

He started down the tunnel but stopped and turned. "What about Madame Leota?"

"What about her? You do not believe in spirits. Therefore, she is a fraud. A charlatan." The librarian handed him a candle for light. "Mind your step, Master William."

William wasn't ready to leave. "You don't understand. I be—" The bookshelf rumbled closed, cutting him off midsentence. He was alone in the corridor, the path leading back to the graveyard. If only he could have learned how Madame Leota communicated with the dead. *Gong!* The chime of a grandfather clock echoed from within the mansion. *Gong!* William was thinking about the stories. *Gong!* The fate of the characters. *Gong!* They were real. *Gong!* As real as his sister. *Gong!* Why couldn't he say her name? *Gong!* The pain had been too great. *Gong!* Now everything was different. *Gong!* The magic was real. *Gong!* Spirits existed. *Gong!* The mansion confirmed it. *Gong!* It was midnight. *Gong!* With unbridled joy, he shouted to any who might be listening: "I believe! I believe!"

With a sudden urgency, William began to run, uncertain where he might end up but knowing full well his final destination would be wondrous, for that was the promise of the mansion itself. "I believe!" He ran through adjoining hallways.

"I believe!" Announcing with a rekindled sense of wonder to the walls that breathed, the portraits that had eyes, the stairs that led to nowhere. To whomever and, more likely, whatever might be listening. "Do you hear me, spirits! I believe!"

William ran through the corridor, shouting for all the happy haunts to hear. "I believe!" He emerged into an unfamiliar setting. William looked around. He was still in the mansion, inside a medium's parlor. A large crystal ball, filled with mist, was floating above a table. He approached and, for the first time, did not question what he saw. "Madame Leota."

The mist inside the ball dissipated, forming a rim of wild blue hair. Then a face appeared, the visage of a handsome lady, surrounded by a phosphorescent glow. "I've been expecting you . . . Billy."

William felt something tug at his heart. He hadn't gone by Billy in ages. His sis had called him that; it was what everyone had called him, all those years before. "These days, I go by William."

The globe settled down in the center of the table, and Madame Leota bade him into the circle. "You may sit." William looked around. "Where? There's no . . ."

A chair glided in from nowhere, settling behind William.

A black raven was perched on the top rail. *Caw! Caw!* "I agree," replied Madame Leota.

"I seek an audience with the dead," William said. The raven was amused, as its cackle would indicate. It still came out sounding like *Caw! Caw! Caw!* "What's so funny?"

"We assumed you hadn't come all this way to play cards," replied Madame Leota. Her complexion changed, her skin turning a luminous green. "It is one thing to seek the dead. Are you prepared to have the dead seek *you*?"

William gave a solemn nod. "I am."

"Very well. State your purpose."

William swallowed hard. That was a tough one. But he knew he had to answer. It was why he had come. "I seek forgiveness." His voice cracked, and she could barely hear him say, "It's my fault . . . she's dead."

Madame Leota's face turned red. "Explain yourself!"

William's eyes grew heavy. "It had to do with a pet, a guinea pig. You see, Chubs was mine and then he was hers, and . . . you're not going to believe this next part."

"I'm a floating head. Try me."

"I see your point." William went on to explain: "According to her friends, my sister made a wish she shouldn't have made. They thought it cost her her life. But what they didn't know was that I made one too. I made a terrible wish. That makes me responsible." William waited for her to respond. "Well, doesn't it?"

"You'll have to ask her," replied the world's most gifted medium. "I require something personal." He withdrew the item from his pocket: a bracelet with four charms representing each of his sister's pets: a rabbit, a parrot, a goldfish, and a guinea pig.

"This was hers."

"Set it down before me." William did as he was told. "Now repeat after me." Leota closed her eyes and spoke the words. **Fair warning, foolish reader. The following spell is 100 percent authentic and has been known to call forth unwanted spirits, the kind that follow you home. Read aloud at your own risk.**

Horntoads and lizards, fiddle and strum. Please answer the roll by beating a drum!

Harpies and furies, old friends and new! Blow on a horn so we'll know that it's you!

Serpents and spiders, tail of a rat. Call in the spirits wherever they're at!

Rap on a table; it's time to respond. Send us a message from somewhere beyond!

Goblins and ghoulies from last Halloween. Awaken the spirits with your tambourine!
Creepies and crawlies, toads in a pond. Let there be music from regions beyond!
Wizards and witches, wherever you dwell, give us a hint by ringing a bell!

The table rumbled and the bracelet floated into the air, charms clinking as it levitated above Leota. William watched the animals turn like a silver carousel. He thought he had seen every trick in the book, but this was different. This was real. "Is it her?" he asked. "Is she here?"

"No!" replied Madame Leota, clearly annoyed.

The bracelet was being tugged back and forth by opposing fields of energy. William watched as if it was an invisible tennis match. "The mischievous monsters have received your sympathetic vibrations and are beginning to materialize," confirmed Madame Leota.

William didn't know whether to laugh or scream as a pair of glowing figures appeared before him. He recognized the two specters having a tug-of-war with his sister's jewelry. They were her pals, members of her storytelling club, the Fearsome Foursome. "I saw it first!" argued Noah, the chubby one.

"Not on your life!" responded Steve, the handsome one. "Unless you want a fatter lip!"

"I'd like to see you try!"

Steve threw a punch Noah's way, and Noah didn't bother to block it. The fist passed directly through his head, as if he was composed of mist. From there, the scuffle continued, forcing Madame Leota to intervene. The crystal ball floated between them. "That's quite enough!" the medium bellowed, and the boys settled down at once. **And if you've ever wondered what scares a ghost, now you know.**

"Escort Billy to the grand ballroom. The direct route. No shortcuts through the attic."

William felt invigorated, like a kid again. He'd waited so long for that day. "I don't know how to thank you."

"Begone!" Madame Leota yelled. Then, with a wink, she added, "You don't want to miss the cake." William turned from the crystal ball and followed the floating apparitions out of the séance circle.

The party was in the grand ballroom. There was a long banquet table, filled with see-through revelers. Ghostly couples were waltzing on the main floor, dancing eternity away, while directly outside, a hearse was dropping off "late arrivals."

Right away, William spotted the guest of honor from the balcony. His sister was twirling ten feet above the dance floor, lighter than air, along with Tim, an apparition in a baseball uniform, who would forever be her favorite partner. They were giggling as they spun, feeling a tickle where their bellies used to be.

As soon as the waltz ended, William ran down the long stairway, passing straight through a string of guests as if they weren't there, though a few protested out of habit: "Hey! Live one! Watch where you're going!"

He spotted her at the head of the banquet table. "Willa!" The guests became silent, and his sister turned her head, looking back, confused. "Don't you know me?" he asked. At first, she didn't. William wasn't a kid anymore. Willa, on the other hand, hadn't aged a day. "Sis, it's me!"

"Billy?" She smiled, just the way he remembered, and for an instant she made her body whole again **(don't ask; it's a ghost thing)**, just long enough to give her little brother a terrestrial hug. "What are you doing here?"

"I came to wish you a happy birthday. And to bring you a present. I missed you, Sis." He held out the bracelet, which she recognized at once. "You never said good-bye," he added as he placed it on her wrist.

"Most people never do."

William bowed his head in shame. "Mostly, I came to apologize."

"What for?"

"I was so mad at you, Will. That night I made a wish, too. I wished . . . well, I wished you wouldn't be around anymore. And just like that, you weren't." He looked into her glowing eyes, still blue, still beautiful. And when Willa looked back, she laughed. Boy, did she laugh!

"You are such a jerkoid. Wishes like that don't come true. What happened to me had nothing to do with you." She touched his cheek and he felt a tingle. "You have to go back, Billy. To live the life you were meant to live."

"No!" Billy shook his head and the other ghosts turned. "I'm staying with you!"

"You can't." And in that moment, he no longer felt Willa's hand. She was merely an apparition once more. A reflection of a being that had once been his sister.

By then, a procession of spirits had floated in around them. Tim, Noah, and Steve, late of the Fearsome Foursome, were carrying a gigantic birthday cake topped with candles. Ghosts swooped down from chandeliers and rafters; a phantom organist played "Happy Birthday" and the guests sang their hearts out. **And their eyes and their lungs and their kidneys.**

At once, William recognized four additional guests: Connie, Uncle Rory and Diana Durwin, and of course Camille, who sang sweeter and louder than all the others. This was where their stories had led them. (The Count had to howl along from a window, as that "no pets" policy was still in effect.) The mansion was their new home. Like Willa, they were eternal residents of the happiest haunt on earth.

William smiled, joining the chorus, and when the song ended, Willa blew out her candles and the cake disappeared. **No wishes, though. Her last one didn't work out so well. Again, see volume one.**

"Happy birthday, Sis," whispered William, and he closed his eyes. It was okay to dream again.

When William opened his eyes, he found himself lying in front of Willa's grave. It was morning; a caretaker and a shivering bloodhound were standing over him. William squinted to see, blocking the sunlight with his hand. "What time is it?"

"Around seven. You sleep here all night?"

"I-I guess so."

The caretaker extended his hand and helped William to his feet. "Just put on a pot of joe, if you're interested."

"Thank you," said William. "A cup of joe sounds like a plan." He didn't know if the entire night had been a dream, but something in his heart knew for certain: Willa was at peace. He checked his jacket. The pocket was empty, and he frantically began searching the grounds.

"You lose something?"

"Yes. A piece of jewelry. I had it in my—" Suddenly, William wasn't talking; he was staring off in amazement.

"You all right, friend?"

"It's Billy, call me Billy. And I'm great. I've never been better!" He was euphoric, laughing for the first time in years. It had to do with Willa's grave. The bracelet, featuring the charms of a rabbit, a parrot, a goldfish, and a guinea pig, had been sculpted into the granite, around the wrist of the stone angel. Which no longer came as a surprise. For William Gaines, the world was once again filled with the unexplainable, the unimaginable.

The magical.

Hereafter Thoughts

Still here, foolish reader?

Congratulations to you and a thousand curses to us!

Like Master William, you made it through in one piece. As much as I'd relish adding you to our carnivorous collection, you have much to accomplish before you "retire." But I admire your spirit. Your willingness to embrace magic in all its forms is what living—and unliving—is all about. So keep on believing in the unbelievable. It just might save your life.

For now.

Until we meet again, foolish mortal, unpleasant dreams. Oh, and . . . hurry back!

BIOGRAPHIES

Amicus Arcane *Little is known about the dearly departed Amicus Arcane, save for his love of books. As the mansion librarian, both in this life and in the afterlife, Amicus has delighted in all forms of the written word. However, this librarian's favorite tales are those of terror and suspense. After all, there is nothing better to ease a restless spirit than a frightfully good ghost story.*

John Esposito *When John Esposito met Amicus Arcane on a midnight stroll through New Orleans Square, he was so haunted by the librarian's tales that he decided to transcribe them for posterity. John has worked in both film and television, on projects such as* Stephen King's Graveyard Shift, R. L. Stine's The Haunting Hour, Teen Titans, *and the* Walking Dead *web series, for which he won consecutive Writer's Guild Awards. John lives in New York with his wife and children and still visits with Amicus from time to time.*

Kelley Jones *For the illustrations accompanying his terrifying tales, Amicus Arcane approached Kelley Jones, an artist with a scary amount of talent. Kelley has worked for every major comic book publisher but is best known for his definitive work on Batman for DC Comics. Kelley lives in Northern California with his wife and children and hears from Amicus every October 31, whether he wants to or not.*

DEAD END!
Prepare to Exit
to the Living World